Marvin Dixon's debut novel, *Settlement*, was published in 2019 inspired by his experiences in the world of financial services. Thus began the story of Justin Kell a financial journalist and private investigator with a passion for ensuring justice is done. *Payback* (2021) and *Redemption* (2022) continued Kell's story with *Brotherly Love* being the fourth in the series.

Now retired from financial services and focussing on his writing, Marvin Dixon lives in West Yorkshire.

For Ange with love

Marvin Dixon

BROTHERLY LOVE

AUSTIN MACAULEY PUBLISHERS™
LONDON • CAMBRIDGE • NEW YORK • SHARJAH

Copyright © Marvin Dixon 2023

The right of Marvin Dixon to be identified as author of this work has been asserted by the author in accordance with sections 77 and 78 of the Copyright, Designs and Patents Act 1988.

All rights reserved. No part of this publication may be reproduced, stored in a retrieval system, or transmitted in any form or by any means, electronic, mechanical, photocopying, recording, or otherwise, without the prior permission of the publishers.

Any person who commits any unauthorised act in relation to this publication may be liable to criminal prosecution and civil claims for damages.

This is a work of fiction. Names, characters, businesses, places, events, locales, and incidents are either the products of the author's imagination or used in a fictitious manner. Any resemblance to actual persons, living or dead, or actual events is purely coincidental.

A CIP catalogue record for this title is available from the British Library.

ISBN 9781398433069 (Paperback)
ISBN 9781398433373 (ePub e-book)

www.austinmacauley.com

First Published 2023
Austin Macauley Publishers Ltd®
1 Canada Square
Canary Wharf
London
E14 5AA

The seed for *Brotherly Love* began with a chat in the car with my eldest son, John, on a trip to Liverpool when he explained the workings of the finance of private schools. The teaching insight came from his brother, Steve, so a real family affair. Thanks guys.

Special thanks go to my brother, Bill, for his critiques, editing and ongoing support. Also to Robin Styles whose insight and feedback was invaluable to telling the tale of the Solomon brothers. It's amazing what you can achieve over a couple of beers.

Cheers, guys, couldn't have done it without you.

Table of Contents

Prologue	**11**
1	**17**
2	**25**
3	**34**
4	**42**
5	**50**
6	**56**
7	**68**
8	**76**
9	**85**
10	**94**
11	**102**
12	**108**
13	**114**
14	**120**
15	**129**
16	**135**
17	**141**

18	146
19	154
20	160
21	167
22	175
23	183
24	191
25	199
26	205
27	211
28	216
29	223
30	229
31	235
32	241
33	248
34	257
35	265
36	271
37	275
Epilogue	279

Prologue

The Four Horsemen sat in their common room each lost in their own thoughts as they mulled over their options. Their end-of-term prank had gone terribly wrong, despite all the planning. What was supposed to be a small, contained fire in a waste bin in the Assembly Hall had quickly gotten out of control due to some idiot trying to be a hero and attempting to throw the burning contents through the open window and onto the Quad.

When some of the paper didn't quite make it and fell back onto the velvet curtains, which in their opinion couldn't have met any of the current fire-resistant safety standards, the ensuing conflagration had left one side of the Congregation Hall a badly charred mess. The wooden panels were alight in seconds despite the sprinkler system immediately kicking in and the smoke damage rendered the 19th-century ceiling adorned with Pre-Raphaelite frescos unrecognisable.

As the acknowledged leader of their little group and architect of the plan to make sure the dreary final assembly of the year didn't go ahead, Roddy broke the silence.

'OK, listen up. We need to get our stories straight and make sure we don't get expelled. It was an accident, that's all. I'll say I was playing around with my lighter and accidentally dropped it in the bin. I tried to get it out, but the bin was full and the paper caught fire.'

'No good,' said Al. 'As soon as you let go of the clicker, the lighter would go out. No one, especially Doc Solomons, would believe you. And of course, there are umpteen witnesses who saw you bending over the bin.'

'Have you got a better idea then?' snapped Roddy, clearly irked by the response of his best friend.

'Calm down, you two, we won't get anywhere by falling out with each other. And let's face it, who gives a shit,' said Con. 'Anyway, we're in this together, that's the covenant we made. We stick together and take whatever punishment they give us. They won't want to piss off our folks and when our parents pay for the damage, we'll just be suspended from some of the summer activities with maybe extra homework thrown in.'

The smug smile on Conor O'Clery's face oozed the sense of entitlement that they all felt. Con was by far the most pragmatic of the four of them. The O'Clerys were one of the wealthiest families in Ireland. His farmer grandfather had the foresight to sell off vast swathes of the land that had been in the family for years for construction, infrastructure projects and renewable energy developments, making sure he had a stake in the ones he thought would be profitable.

When his father inherited the sizeable portfolio, he had the sense to have a hands-on approach to overseeing all aspects of the business and not to expose his interests to any unnecessary risks. To Patrick O'Clery the annual fees of £45,000 to keep his only son at the prestigious Wellington public school in the Hertfordshire countryside was a mere drop in the proverbial ocean.

'I don't care what happens, in fact I hope we do get expelled. I didn't really fancy spending the summer in this dump anyway,' interjected Max. 'This secret group of ours is something for Year Sevens, I mean "The Four Horsemen", come on, we need to grow up.'

His three friends stared at Maksim Orlov, dumbstruck.

Roddy stood up and started pacing the around the room.

'You can't mean that Max, we all agreed we're in this till we leave next year with whatever shitty A levels we can manage to pass. We've got to bring down that bastard Solomons, he's been on our case since day one. He deserves what he's got coming!'

'And what exactly is that?' asked Max.

'We have to get him out of this school for the benefit of all those poor little rich kids that follow in our footsteps. That man's evil and it's our job to expose him,' replied Roddy.

Realising that his friend had started one of his ranting monologues, Con interrupted, 'Just because he lives with his mother in a big house in the countryside doesn't make him evil Roddy. A bit strange maybe, but not evil. OK, he's been quite harsh with the detentions and making fools of us in his boring English Lit classes, but he's not some demon with horns, that can only be challenged by the four horsemen of the Apocalypse. And I agree with Max, it was OK to have this secret club when we came here five years ago, but we start Year 13 in September, we'll be old enough to vote soon, we're not kids anymore.'

'I'm with Roddy on this,' said Al. 'Doc Solomons is not a nice person and I'm all for making his life as uncomfortable as possible while we're still here. It doesn't matter what we call ourselves so long as we finish what we started.'

The conversation ended abruptly when Doctor Bill Solomons calmly walked into the common room with a big smile on his face. 'Gentlemen, if you could come with me please, you have some explaining to do.'

*

Principal Mark Smith convened a meeting of the School's Executive team as soon as the fire brigade had confirmed the Congregation Hall was safe and it was simply a case of starting the clean-up. Smith's attitude to the latest hiatus was reflected in his appearance.

His tattered tweed suit, the worn collar of his unbuttoned shirt and school tie hanging at half-mast around his neck painted a picture of a man who was at the end of his tether. His two deputies along with each faculty Head were in attendance nervously twiddling their pens and pencils. The only matter to discuss was what to do about the perpetrators of the fire and the practicalities of repairing the damaged Assembly Hall.

'Let's get straight to the matter in hand,' said Smith. 'Bill, over to you. You were on duty in the Hall when the fire started, what can you tell us?'

Bill Solomons was Head of English and Religious Studies. He'd been at the school for ten years and was one of the longest-serving staff members.

'I didn't actually see the fire being started, although we know the origin was in one of the metal wastepaper bins that are scattered around the Hall. There was a commotion on the Quad side of the Hall and I saw Goulding, one of the Prefects trying to throw the bin through the window and onto the Quad.

Some of the lighted paper fell back onto the curtain which immediately caught fire.

The fire then spread to the wooden panels on the wall. The sprinkler system kicked in and after a few minutes, the fire was put out. When the fire brigade arrived, they confirmed there was no danger of any reignition and no structural damage.'

'Should I ask if we know what the cause of the fire was?' asked Smith.

'Various eyewitnesses claim they saw Roderick Roan putting paper into the bin whilst playing with a cigarette lighter. His intolerable friends, Alexander Stewart, Maksim Orlov and Connor O'Clery were with him at the time.'

'Could it have been an accident?' asked Smith.

Before Solomons could answer, Marsha Taylor, one of the Deputy Heads replied, 'Come on, Mark, we all know it wasn't an accident. Roan and his little gang have been nothing but trouble since the day they got here. This is another of their stupid pranks, only this time it could have been fatal. They should all be expelled immediately.'

'I couldn't agree more,' said Solomons.

'But what about proof, due process, evidence. We can't just summarily expel them. What about their parents?' Smith didn't sound convincing and they all knew what was coming next.

'I knew it,' said Solomons. 'It's all about the money and the influence these parents have on the school. Every time one of their little darlings steps out of line our illustrious leader manages to secure another donation to refit the sports hall or buy some more tablets. It's outrageous.'

'That was uncalled for Bill, but sadly it is true. I'm just being practical. The school's finances are in pretty bad shape and the intake of Year Sevens for September is the lowest it has ever been. We can't afford to lose the £180,000 fees that these four boys will provide for next year. So, punish them, yes, but it's not expulsion.'

'Now, both of you, just hang on a minute.' This time it was the other Deputy Barney Thompson. 'We haven't even heard what they've got to say for themselves. And you keep talking about the four of them when apparently, it was only Roan who was directly involved.'

Principal Smith cut a pathetic figure as he put his head in his hands at the end of the table. It was all getting too much for him. Finally, he looked up.

'Right, Bill, Marsha and Barney, you can carry out whatever investigation you think is appropriate and report back next week, so we can collectively decide on an appropriate punishment, but it won't be expelling them. The four of them are summer boarders so I'm sure we can be creative. I'll take forward the repairs and contact the parents. And, before you ask, yes, I will get donations that more than cover the costs. Thank you, meeting over.'

1

Saul Solomons looked at his watch and sighed inwardly when the digital readout showed 04:39. He'd been in the casino playing roulette for nearly nine hours and the winning streak that started just before midnight had run out an hour ago and he was down to his last £50. Five ten pound chips and the decision of where to place them.

The fact he had an important 9 o'clock meeting in a little over four hours didn't cross his mind as he placed the five round discs on his five favourite numbers. 2, 3, 4, 14 and 31. A win wouldn't get his losses back for the evening, but it would at least stake him for the following night, for which there was no doubt he'd be returning.

The mood of the casino was completely different at this time of the morning. When he'd arrived yesterday evening, the players had that optimistic air about them that tonight their luck was going to be in. There was an alertness and anticipation as players and staff moved with purpose. The floor was alive with energy and there was the hubbub of talk and laughter as bets were placed and chips were won and lost.

Of course, as the evening turned into night, which quickly became the early morning, the hope turned slowly into despair. He found himself laughing as he realised that anyone still here at nearly five o'clock in the morning must be desperate. Like him.

There were small groups watching the play with bleary eyes, sipping mugs of tea and coffee, their funds having run out long ago. He didn't understand why they stayed in the dismal purgatory. Maybe it was just to get a little bit of hope that some lucky person did actually win and when they came back tomorrow it would be their turn. For coming back tomorrow was the only certainty in their one-dimensional lives.

He watched the ball as it initially sped round the wheel and as it slowly started bouncing from one number to another, he held his breath, praying to Tyche, the Greek God of Chance.

He barely heard the croupier say, "eighteen red", as he slipped off his stool and headed for the exit. He was already doing the sums in his head of how much headroom he had on his overdraft and the number of days to payday, but for now, he needed to get home and grab a couple of hours of sleep before heading to work.

He smiled and said good morning to the staff who got in early to avoid the crush on the tube as he walked to his office which looked down onto Leadenhall Street in the City of London.

His sleep had been fitful and he felt like he had sand in his eyes. He hoped the banana and two cans of Red Bull he'd had for breakfast would eventually kick in and get him through to lunchtime.

No sooner had he taken his jacket off and started up his laptop, when the boss, Adrian Collins, put his head around the door. 'Morning Saul, glad you're in early, can you pop down to my office for a catch-up before the Audit Committee, Trevor and I have a couple of questions on your report we'd like to be clear on in case the non-execs have any left field questions.'

'Of course, be right down.'

He grabbed the papers for the meeting and walked the short distance to the corner office where Trevor Beaumont, the finance director, was bent over his tablet, presumably doing some last-minute preparation of his own.

Despite his feeling of utter exhaustion, Saul confidently talked through the questions they had on the new Risk Management Framework he was proposing the bank invested in, which would replace various standalone systems, some of which still required manual intervention. He knew he was one of the best in his field of compliance regulation and risk management and to have been appointed to the board last year at the tender age of thirty-nine had even caused his mother to congratulate him, a rare event indeed.

The Audit Committee dragged on for three hours and despite numerous cups of black coffee, he barely managed to stay awake. He was able to contribute at the right points, answer the questions that were asked of him and even have a chat with the Chairman at the end of the meeting. But as he got in the lift to take him back to the second floor and his office, all he wanted to do was sleep.

'Please hold all calls, Jane,' he said to his PA. 'I don't want to be disturbed for the next hour,' he said as he shut the door of his office and slumped into one of the chairs around the small meeting table. He rested his head in the crook of his left arm and immediately fell asleep.

Forty minutes later, he became aware of a buzzing and then a ringing noise which slowly brought him back to consciousness. Just as he came to and realised where he was, it stopped. His body was telling him to put his head back down and continue the bliss of sleep, but realising he was in his office and not being sure how long he'd been out, he stirred himself and started stretching the aches from his neck and shoulders.

Fortunately, no one important had wanted to see him, so he poured himself a cup of coffee from the percolator that Jane kept regularly topped up and checked his mobile that had brought him out of his slumbers. There was a missed call and a voicemail. He tapped to play the message as he sat down at his desk and woke up his laptop.

'Hi, Saul, it's Markita from Executive Search, I've got good news on the job with Streem Bank, they'd like to see you for an initial chat tomorrow evening at six thirty if you can make it. Please, can you call me back as soon as you can to confirm. Thanks.'

Saul found himself smiling as he clicked off the call. He'd kept in touch with Markita since she'd got him his current role three years ago. She was always ringing up to ask him if he'd be interested in moving on to another "opportunity" that had just come on the market and he'd always said no. That was until a couple of weeks ago when the job at Streem had come up.

His first thought before he agreed to any business or social engagement outside of working hours was how would it affect his time at the casino. Six thirty on a Friday was the start of the weekend and he'd planned to head straight to the Rupert's to get on his favourite table while it was quiet, subject that was to finding some funds to play with of course. But what would probably only be a half-hour chat over a cup of coffee wouldn't delay him too much, so he rang Markita back, got the details and confirmed he'd be there.

The job at Streem was the Money Laundering Reporting Officer position. He undertook this responsibility as part of his current role, but as the regulations got tougher, more banks were separating out the MLRO job, mainly because of the creative ways criminals were finding to launder their dirty money. Streem was a relatively new bank, coming to market two years ago.

Like the majority of new enterprises, they didn't have any branch network other than in their Head Office in Farringdon. The important thing from Saul's perspective was they were offering more money than he was currently earning and there was always a chance of a golden hello.

He put all thoughts of the interview out of his mind and turned his attention to the more pressing matter of the state of his finances. He logged into online banking and saw that he had £143 headroom on his overdraft. He could go beyond his limit, but the charges were excessive and would do even more damage to his credit rating.

He had one credit card that was maxed out and he didn't get paid till next Thursday. He needed to buy food for the week and there was no point going to the casino with less than £100. There was only one option. He opened the contacts on his mobile, scrolled down to "Mother" and dialled.

Esther Solomons did not own a mobile phone. She never understood why people would want to carry a phone that meant anyone could ring them at any time of the day or night. She'd had to be persuaded by the boys to put a second phone in her bedroom, only relenting a couple of years ago as she'd got less mobile and kept missing calls when the housekeeper wasn't there and she couldn't get downstairs in time. She also wouldn't entertain an answering machine. If anyone wanted to speak to her, then they would simply have to ring back.

In recent years, her housekeeper, Mrs Buckle, had become more of a personal assistant, dealing with the small amount of mail she still received, acting as a chauffeur and passing on instructions to the gardener.

She had a small number of friends who she socialised with. This mainly consisted of fortnightly visits to each other's houses for afternoon tea and the odd evening playing bridge, but she was content enough with having William still living with her. The eldest of her two sons, William as she insisted on calling him, provided a reassuring presence since her husband had died last year. The house was large enough that each had their own space, but they generally ate their evening meals together and there was always plenty of conversation from the school as well as the news items of the day.

She was in her kitchen preparing the vegetables for that night's meal when the phone rang. She knew the call could only be from a handful of people but had a good idea who it would be.

'Esther Solomons.'

'Hello, mother, it's Saul, how are you?'

'Ah, Saul, how good to hear from you. I'm very well, just preparing the evening meal for William. Are you ringing to say you'll be joining us?'

'Sorry, I'm very busy at work at the moment. How is Bill, I haven't spoken to him for a few weeks.'

'He's very well. Looking forward to the end of term, although he rang me earlier to say he'd be late home this evening as there has been a fire in the main Hall. No one was hurt, thank goodness, but he's looking into what happened. Anyway, what I can do for you? Is it money you want?'

Saul cringed as his mother got straight to the point.

'Well, yes, actually, it is. Just a thousand until I get paid next week.'

'You always say that and according to my records, you have never paid anything back when you get paid. I don't know what you do with your money.'

She paused, waiting to hear what the excuse would be this time.

'I'm waiting for a return on an investment I'm involved with. It's taking longer than we thought for things to get going. I'll pay you everything back in a few months, I promise.'

Saul was ashamed of how easily the lies came these days. And lying to his mother was as low as you could go.

'Thirteen thousand five hundred pounds is what I've given you in the last two years, with only five hundred being paid back. You're saying that you can repay this in full in three months' time?' Her voice had taken on a harder tone which he didn't like the sound of.

'Definitely by the end of the year, yes. I promise mother and this will be the last time I ask you for anything.'

'I doubt that very much, but alright, I'll transfer the money tomorrow. This means fourteen thousand to be repaid by 31 December.'

'Thanks, mother, I really appreciate this.'

'Anyway, enough of money. When are you coming to see us? Soon, I hope.'

'I'm busy for the next couple of weekends, so hopefully after that.' Saul knew not to be too specific.

'Very well, I look forward to confirming the date. Now unless there's anything else, I've got vegetables to prepare. Goodbye.'

As the call ended, Saul breathed a sigh of relief. The money should see him through the weekend and if he happened to win big, he'd stop playing and put some of the winnings to one side. He knew his mother would keep to her word and that he'd certainly used the last of any goodwill there was from her. He knew he needed a fresh start which didn't involve gambling, so he'd see how the next week went and then take stock.

The world would seem a better place once he'd had some sleep and as he didn't have funds to gamble with, for the first time in ages he'd have a night off. He was surprised at how good he felt as he walked out of the office and headed to Bank to catch the DLR. Maybe there was hope for him after all he thought, *Yes maybe there was.*

2

Esther Solomons ended the call with her youngest son and openly sighed. She worried about Saul and the financial problems he clearly had. It wasn't that she minded helping him out from time to time, but his requests for money were becoming more and more frequent.

He had a good job at the bank, had recently been promoted to the board and didn't indulge in fancy cars or expensive holidays. He'd split from his partner two years ago and there weren't any children involved, so where did all his money go? When she tried to discuss it with William, he simply shrugged his shoulders, clearly indicating he didn't care.

She knew that both her sons were surprised and angry that their father had not left them anything in his will. The houses, the car, the share portfolio and various investments had all been left to her. At the recent reading of the will, they had been shocked that their father hadn't left anything to them, saying that he'd verbally promised them cash and various personal possessions.

There had been several family rows and the threat of them contesting it still hung in the air. Whenever Saul rang, she was always relieved when the matter didn't come up, grateful to keep him happy by agreeing to the now regular requests for money.

Her thoughts were disturbed by the sound of car tyres coming up the gravel driveway and turning toward the east wing of the house where William lived. The house wasn't really big enough to refer to the two halves as an east and west wing, but this was how the estate agent had described it when she'd bought it with her husband all those years ago.

There was a separate entrance to where William lived and he had two bedrooms, one with an ensuite, a separate bathroom, a good-sized lounge, a small study and a kitchen which was big enough to hold a table that could seat six people. This configuration was replicated on the other side where Esther lived, with a large hall providing the demarcation line.

They had not thought it necessary to preclude access to their individual space when William moved in, so both could freely move about the family home. Despite the proximity, they only met for dinner when William wasn't attending a function at the school and decided to stay over in the small bedroom that all teachers were provided with.

She was surprised when he came straight into her kitchen, dumped his ageing brown leather briefcase on the floor and pulled a bottle of Rioja out of the wine rack.

'I don't need to ask if you had a good day then. Was anyone hurt in the fire?'

'Bloody terrible day! Damn kids set fire to a waste bin in the Main Hall, all sorts of damage done and muggins here is in charge of the investigation.'

'But was anyone hurt?' repeated Esther.

'No, thank goodness. They're saying it was an accident, but I know it was deliberate.' He took a deep gulp of his wine.

'Why would anyone want to intentionally start a fire in the Hall on the last day of term?'

'Because they're evil, little bastards and because they hate me.'

'I assume it's the same gang you've had trouble with before?'

'Yes, they've got it in for me and know that I'm powerless to do anything about it. Even Mark admits we need their fees as the school is struggling, so he won't sanction expelling them. He actually hopes the parents will pay more than is needed for the repairs, so we'll profit from it!'

Esther knew better than to say anything and just let him continue with his usual rant about his profession.

'The trouble is teaching was once regarded amongst professions, such as doctors and lawyers, but now we are just the butt of people's jokes. As everyone has been through education, they believe it gives them the right to give you their two pennies worth on what they think of schools and us educators, even when you never asked them to. This is even worse in a place like ours where the parents are paying for the privilege.

If I was in a courtroom, I would never dream of telling a lawyer or solicitor how I think the legal system should work or how they should do their job. I've been in hospital, but I wouldn't sit the surgeon down and speak to him about the issues facing the nation due to the poor health care system.

The problem is being a teacher is so relatable to everyone and all I get from these self-made millionaires is "school never taught me anything". What they forget is that we teach their kids how to think, not what to think. Anyway, I'm at my wit's end, that's it. I'm going to spend the summer deciding what I'm going to do next. If I had my share of father's money, I could start my own business, but there's no chance of that is there?'

Esther had heard similar monologues on numerous occasions. They had become the norm, particularly when her eldest had had a bad day. Normally he would have calmed down by the morning, but this time, it was more intense, more vitriolic.

'Do you have to go in tomorrow?' she asked.

'No, not until Monday. I interviewed them with Barney and Marsha this afternoon and we're leaving them to stew over the weekend. We report back to our pathetic Principal on Monday and recommend an appropriate punishment.'

'What did they have to say for themselves?'

'Roan, the one who started the fire said his lighter accidentally fell into the bin and must have still been alight. The other three said they were fooling around and it was definitely an accident. The other pupils are reluctant to comment, although one of the prefects is certain he saw Roan putting paper into the bin and then bending over it and whoosh!'

'It doesn't matter anyway. The four of them are staying for the summer, so it'll just be a case of some extra coursework and maybe cleaning some of the dorms.'

He drained his glass and poured himself another large measure.

'The one I'm concerned about is Roan, he's the ringleader and a strange one. He often starts quoting religious texts in lessons where it's completely irrelevant and will take to walking around in his bare feet. When we have reading sessions, he always reads aloud. It's only a murmur but is very disconcerting. The others think it's hilarious, but my view is he's a disturbed young man.'

'What do the other teachers think?'

'Just that he's trying to wind them up, attention seeking. They just ignore it. Right, I'm going for a shower, what time will dinner be ready?'

'Three-quarters of an hour, I'm just about to put the chicken in.'

Bill finished his wine and nodded to his mother. She watched him go, now worrying about not just one but both of her children.

Bill often wondered how he'd ended up as a forty-one-year-old frustrated teacher living with his mother. In the twenty years since he'd left Oxford, he'd changed from an optimistic graduate who was going to change the world, to a frustrated English and RE teacher who detested himself for what he'd become.

He felt like a raindrop slowly making its way down a windowpane, randomly changing its course to find the easiest route to the bottom. Making a journey that no one really cared about, especially the raindrop itself. He'd drifted for the last twenty years always going with the flow, taking the easy option, never taking the tough decisions that would probably have made him a better person.

It started when he met Caroline at the start of his final year at Oxford. She was studying politics and economics and had a job lined up in the Home Office after she graduated. She was beautiful, funny, dynamic and single-minded. What Caroline wanted; Caroline got.

Their love for each other grew throughout that year and she convinced him to scrap his plans to stay on for his Masters and follow her to London. Like the raindrop on the windowpane, he simply took the easiest course and they moved into a bedsit in Brent Cross. Teaching was the obvious option and he got as a job as a teaching assistant whilst he studied for his PGCE.

Things started to turn sour between them eighteen months later. He's got a job at the local secondary school and was actually enjoying the challenge of his first proper teaching position, trying to influence the lives of the pupils he taught. Caroline had been promoted twice by then and their lives were physically and emotionally drifting apart.

Her long hours and weekend work meant they seldom enjoyed any quality time together until eventually, she decided it was over. He could see the end coming but just waited for her to make the decision. And of course, she did. She moved into a flat in central London with two women from her department and he kept the bedsit for which he couldn't afford the rent. At the end of the academic year, he handed in his notice and moved back to the family home for the summer to decide what he'd do next.

Teaching jobs were easy to come by and took a position at a secondary school in Enfield. He found himself a small flat near the school but was still close enough to the family home to go there at weekends with his washing and for Sunday lunch. Once again, the easy option and another move towards the bottom of the windowpane.

After a year, he got promoted to the number two in the department and twelve months after that he was the Head of English when the incumbent resigned to go travelling! Back then he didn't understand why a thirty-year-old would want to see the world. But now, he did.

It was at this time he started seeing Anne, one of the admin assistants in the school office. They'd got to know each other at various social events the staff organised and then started going out for a drink on their own on a Friday. Anne was divorced, a couple of years older and had two young children. They all got on so well that six months later he moved in.

A readymade family, a nice house, although it was quite small and someone who he believed he could spend the rest of the life with. The perfect life!

The marriage was the following summer and they moved to a larger semi-detached that was closer to Anne's mum's so she could help more with the childcare.

It was easy for him to simply drift along and take another turn to the bottom of the windowpane.

In his mind, the inevitable happened a couple of years later. Problems at work, problems with kids, whom he wasn't allowed to discipline, problems with Anne's mum and the arguments that would start over the slightest thing. Working together became almost impossible, so he took the easy option. He resigned and went back to the family home a bitter and resentful man.

It was one of his mother's friends, (of course) that had connections at the Wellington School and being just a few miles from the family home was the obvious next step in his career. Maybe the children of wealthy parents would be less obnoxious and more interested in their education that those he'd encountered to date. By and large they were, although the likes of Roderick Roan and his friends were some of the exceptions.

And here he still was, living at home waiting for someone to come along and make his next decision for him. Little did he know it would happen sooner than he thought and from a most unexpected source.

*

Roddy Roan sat on his bed in the small dormitory were he and his three friends slept. The dorm had six beds, but the lack of pupils in the school were such that two remained empty. He was on his own and reading one of his favourite passages from the book of Revelation. As usual, his voice spoke the words just above a whisper.

Then I saw the Lamb break open the first of the seven seals and I heard one of the four living creatures say in a voice that sounded like thunder, 'Come!' I looked and there was a white horse. Its rider held a bow and he was given a crown. He rode out as a conqueror to conquer.

Then the Lamb broke open the second seal and I heard the second living creature say, 'Come!' Another horse came out, a red one. Its rider was given the power to bring war on the earth so that people should kill each other. He was given a large sword.

Then the Lamb broke open the third seal and I heard the third living creature say, 'Come!' I looked and there was a black horse. Its rider held a pair of scales in his hand. I heard what sounded like a voice coming from among the four living creatures, which said, 'A litre of wheat for a day's wages and three litres of barley for a day's wages. But do not damage the olive trees and the vineyards!'

Then the Lamb broke open the fourth seal and I heard the fourth living creature say, 'Come!' I looked and there was a pale-coloured horse. Its rider was named Death and Hades followed close behind. They were given authority over a quarter of the earth, to kill by means of war, famine, disease and wild animals.

He stopped reading and closed his eyes, turning his head towards the Heavens.

'Yes, the Apocalypse and I will make it happen.'

3

It was seven thirty when Saul walked through the door of his small flat in Shadwell. He threw his man bag on the kitchen table, staggered into the bedroom, slumped onto the bed and immediately fell asleep. It was one of those rare occasions when his body overruled the adrenalin of his addiction and insisted it got some rest. It didn't happen often, but he'd only managed a handful of hours in his bed in the last fortnight and with the stress of his precarious financial position and desperately trying to maintain a veneer of professionalism at work, his body had finally said enough is enough.

His sleep was deep, dreamless and lasted for eleven hours before being broken by the ringing of his phone. He slowly dragged himself back to consciousness and stopped the alarm which showed it was 06:30. Once he'd showered, he felt completely refreshed and excited at the prospects for the coming day. He had a clear diary, so no tedious meetings to sit through. An interview for a potential new job and with the money from his mother, a night at the casino to look forward to. The outlook could not have been better.

He picked up his breakfast at the Pret round the corner from the office and settled into the porridge and coffee sitting at his desk. He decided it would be best to do some prep ahead of his meeting at Streem, so he began by checking out the CEO and the board on the various sources that made everybody's life so transparent.

First, he checked the PRA register to establish names and responsibilities and then went on LinkedIn to review their profiles and to see if there was any common ground. He found the usual stereotypical careers, with spells at finance houses, banks and even the regulators and whilst there were some names he recognised from industry forums and articles in the trade press, he didn't actually know any of them personally.

Finally, he searched for the person who he would be replacing. Emile Black was deregistered with the Prudential Regulation Authority last month but hadn't updated his LinkedIn profile which was unusual as people tended to want to shout about their new jobs and success in finding a better role. Anyway, it was only an initial chat and he had the basics of what he needed.

His mood brightened even more when just before lunchtime an alert on his phone confirmed that the money from his mother had gone into his account. He'd decided to take £500 in cash with him that evening and only draw on the other £500 if absolutely necessary. He wanted to get back to the days when if he'd achieved a certain amount of winnings, he'd stop, walk away from the table, bank the surplus and then return the next time to start again. He couldn't actually recall the last time he'd managed to do this, maybe a couple of years ago? Nowadays, wild dogs couldn't drag him away from a winning streak.

It was a lovely summers day, so he decided he'd get a sandwich and walk down to the river to enjoy the sunshine.

As he picked up his phone to head out, it rang, with a caller ID that he didn't often get.

'Hi, Bill, to what do I owe the pleasure?' he asked his brother.

'Straight to the point as usual. I'm feeling shit thank you very much, how are you doing?'

'Oh dear, you haven't had another row with mother have you?'

'That's part of the problem, but there's also a lot of bad stuff going on at the school and I'm thinking of jacking it in. Can you come up this weekend, we need to talk.'

Saul was surprised by the pleading tone of his big brother. There was only a couple of years between them, but it always felt a lot more than that. 'Er, I'm busy this weekend, but I'm free for a good chat now if that works?'

There was a long pause before Bill replied, 'OK, I'll give you the headlines, but we must meet in the next couple of weeks. I've got some decisions to make.'

Saul shut the door of his office and settled back in his chair. 'Go ahead, I'm all ears.'

'I don't know where to start, but the root of the problem is the school. I'm not happy there, I hate most of the kids and the teachers and the Principal is a pathetic wimp. The school's also in financial trouble and there's rumours it may be sold and I'm not sure I could stand the scrutiny of a new board assessing whether I'm up to the job.'

'So, why don't you just leave? There must be plenty of teaching jobs around or simply take some time out, have a gap year like the students do.'

'It's not as easy as that. I'm embarrassed that I still live at home. I want to move out, move on but I also want my share of father's money. I want to make a fresh start away from here before I do something I'll regret.'

The desperation in his brother's voice made Saul realise there was something badly wrong with his older sibling.

'What do you mean by doing something you'll regret?'

Another long pause ensued while Bill thought whether he should share his dark thoughts with his brother.

'Let's leave that till we meet. If you can't come up this weekend, how about a week on Sunday? We can meet in the Oak, have a couple of beers and then go to the house for lunch and tackle mother together.'

Despite his reluctance to leave London and potentially a Saturday night, Sunday morning session at the tables, he sensed it was important to agree for his brother's sake.

'OK, one thirty at the Oak a week Sunday and you can buy.'

'Thanks, Saul, see you then.'

He put his phone down and sat for a couple of minutes wondering about the problems his brother was clearly having. It was the first time since their father's death that they'd had anything coming close to a personal conversation, which was a concern in itself. Anyway, there was nothing he could do about it until they met, so he set off to enjoy his lunch hour in the sunshine.

*

He arrived at Streem at exactly six thirty and was met in the Reception area by an attractive woman in her thirties who introduced herself as the HR director.

'Thanks for coming to see us this evening Saul, I'm Suzie Canning, Head of HR.'

'No problem at all,' replied Saul, as he followed her to the lifts.

'It'll just be Abebe and myself this evening. We prefer not to be too formal here and everyone is referred to by their first names, even the CEO.'

Saul knew that Abebe Bah was the driving force behind the launch of Streem Bank and was credited with its rapid growth in the last few years. He'd set up various banks in his native West Africa before coming to the UK to take advantage of the government's desire to create more competition in the banking sector.

They emerged from the lift onto the main floor of the office and he followed Suzie through the standard open-plan layout and onto a corridor of individual offices. The door of the second one was open and she led him into what he thought was modest accommodation for a CEO.

He was met by a smiling Abebe Bah and invited to sit at one of the three seats set around the meeting table in the centre of the room.

Abebe Bah was an imposing figure. A shade over six feet, he just about got away with the extra pounds he'd started to put on in the last couple of years. His back hair was neatly cut and his eyes had a sharp intensity that made you reluctant to meet his gaze. His dark blue tailored suit was impeccable, although the absence of a tie softened his overall look.

'Welcome to Streem, Saul and thanks for coming to see us on a Friday evening. I hope you haven't had to change any plans,' Abebe enquired in a voice that had a breathy timbre.

'It's my pleasure,' replied Saul. 'I'm meeting some friends later, so this fits in perfectly well, thanks.'

'Good, now I've read your CV and can see you have the experience, expertise and qualifications that I'm looking for, so this is simply a casual chat to see if you are a good fit for the organisation. So, tell me something about yourself that isn't on the CV.'

Saul was surprised by the approach and momentarily panicked as all he could think about was his alternative career in gambling.

'Well, er, I've always been quite sporty, but my work life has meant I haven't had much opportunity to play my golf and football. I've got a brother who teaches in a private school in Hertfordshire and I try to get to see him at least once a month. If the weather's good, we may have a game of golf but it's usually just a nice long lunch.'

'Which school does he teach at?' asked Abebe.

'The Wellington, he's the Head of English.'

'Very good and why do you want to come and work for Streem?'

'Well, I've known Markita at Executive Search for a few years and she knows I'm looking for my next move, so when she got in touch I was really excited at coming to talk to you about the opportunity.'

'And why are you so excited?' Abebe's voice took on a more formal tone.

'Where I am at the moment is a more traditional bank. It's quite risk-averse and it doesn't really challenge me anymore. From what I've read Streem is more entrepreneurial and that's the type of organisation I want to work for. Oh and you're offering more money.'

Saul smiled hoping he'd struck the right note.

'We are a forward-looking organisation, which is why we take great care finding the right people.' The CEO had regained his charming, relaxed persona. 'Suzie, over to you.'

The HR Director ran through the boringly standard questions about his career he'd expected, which he answered despite the details being on his CV that she was reading from. He answered politely and managed to ask a couple of what he thought were relevant questions of his own.

Finally, she said, 'That's everything from me. Abebe, is there anything else from you.'

Abebe Bah simply shook his head.

'And Saul, anything further you'd like to ask?'

'Just one final thing, Emile Black, has he gone to another firm or to another role in the organisation?' asked Saul.

Saul noticed a brief exchange in the looks between his two interviewers.

'He left for personal reasons,' replied Suzie. 'So, if you've no more questions we'll get back to the agency next week and take it from there.'

Suzie Canning led him to the lift making the usual small talk and then headed back to the office for the debrief with the boss.

Abebe had moved back to his desk and was studying his phone when she sat down in front of him.

'What did you think of our Mr Solomons then?' he asked.

'He's certainly capable of doing the job and more importantly fits the profile we're looking for.'

'Yes, I agree. His background is such that it won't be any problem getting him registered with the PRA and his financial position should make it easy for us to motivate him. Do we have any more details on that?'

'He's a member of the Rupert's Casino and he goes there at least six nights a week. You don't need to be Einstein to understand why his credit rating is so poor.'And the family?' asked Abebe.

'It's as he said. He does have a brother who teaches at the Wellington and his mother is a very wealthy widow. I'd say he's exactly what we're looking for.'

'Good, get him in front of the rest of the board next week and move to appoint him as soon as possible. What do you think about him asking about Emile?'

'It's a standard question that most candidates ask. When he gets here, all he'll hear is the personal reasons strapline. It won't be an issue,' she replied.

'Thank you, Suzie. Now go and start enjoying your weekend.'

Saul Solomons headed across town to his appointment with the roulette table with a spring in his step. The interview couldn't have gone any better and he was sure the attractive Suzie has taken a shine to him! Tonight was going to be a lucky night, of that he was sure.

4

'Justin Kell's office, Molly speaking. How can I help you?'

Kell looked up from his laptop and smiled to himself at how far Molly had come in the twelve months since the Mandara investigation. They were now a true partnership both professionally and personally. The horrors of her experience at the hands of the psychopath Jimmy Skaa a distant memory.

'Hi, Chris, good to hear from you. How's life up in Manchester?'

Kell listened with interest to one end of the conversation as it could only be his ex-colleague and good friend Chris Packham on the other end of the line.

'Yes, he's here, I'll transfer you now. Good to speak to you, Chris. Take care.'

Kell and Packham exchanged the usual pleasantries as they caught up on what each other was up to, which was basically work in Packham's case.

'How are you and Moly getting along, she sounds happy?' Packham asked.

Conscious that Molly was no doubt taking in everything he said, Kell was cautious in his reply. 'All good thanks, in fact better than good. The business is really thriving. We're turning away work at the moment.'

'You can fill in me on the juicy bits when we meet. I'm in London next week and as well as catching up properly, there's something I want to talk through. Are you around Monday or Tuesday evening?'

'Sounds intriguing. Tuesday is better for me. Shall we say 7.30 at the usual place?'

'Perfect,' replied Packham. 'I'll pay even though it is your turn! See you then.'

As the call ended, Molly enquired, 'What was all that about then?'

'Chris is down here next week and it sounds like he wants to talk business. We're meeting on Tuesday after work.'

'Am I invited?'

'I think Chris wants to see me on my own. Anyway, it's your Pilates class on Tuesdays.'

'I'm only joking, it'll be good for you to go out without me. It doesn't happen very often, does it?' She smiled as she spoke and Kell marvelled at how mature she was at the tender age of twenty-three. She wasn't clingy and didn't seem bothered by the fifteen-year age difference. She had her own social life and was happy on those rare occasions when he met up with friends or was working late on a job.

Despite the fact they'd been together for twelve months, they hadn't moved in together. They had separate flats both in Leytonstone with Molly sharing with her best friend Luci. She tended to stay at Kell's at the weekend, but neither was pushing to set up home together. Everything was relaxed and casual and was working out just fine.

He glanced at his watch. 'Right come on let's pack up and start the weekend. It's nearly 5 o'clock, so let's head for that new wine bar in Spitalfields and then decide where we're going to eat.'

It was only a five-minute walk from the office on Brick Lane and they managed to find a table near the bar and were soon settled with their drink, deciding to share a bottle of New Zealand Pinot Noir.

'What do you think Chris wants?' asked Molly.

'Mmm, not sure. He clearly didn't want to talk about it on the phone and if he's coming down to London, then it must be something to do with work.'

'Maybe he has a big case he wants us to get involved with. It would make a nice change having something exciting to work on.' She grinned as she said it and Kell knew it was a gentle dig for the fact that she perceived he did all the sleuthing while she focused on the background and technical work.

'I thought you liked all the computer stuff, tracking down assets and background checks.'

'I do, but it's not like when we went up to Manchester last year. That was exciting.'

'The world of organised crime is very dangerous. People get killed, in fact there were a number of deaths if you remember.' Kell's tone was light, as he'd had a number of close shaves himself and wanted Molly to know it was anything but glamorous.

'Anyway,' he continued, 'the Mandara case put an end to any more involvement in that type of work. It's too dangerous so we'll leave it to the likes of Chris and his lot. Now, how about we eat here, fancy ordering some Tapas?'

They spent the rest of the evening making plans for the weekend, before finally heading to Liverpool Street to catch the Central Line home when the mad rush out of the city had quietened down.

'Fancy coming to mine for a nightcap?' Molly asked as they exited the station. 'Luci's in tonight and I'm sure she'd appreciate the company.'

'Sure, but just one mind you. I'm in the gym at eight in the morning,' replied Kell.

They arrived at Molly's five minutes later and settled in the kitchen, deciding that decaf tea was a better option than something stronger. Luci looked a bit on edge and kept glancing at Molly as if she was waiting for her to say something.

'OK, stop looking at me like that, Luci. It's your news so you tell it.'

Kell wondered what on earth was going on until Luci said, 'I'm moving in with my boyfriend at the end of the month, so we've given notice on the flat.' She blurted it out as though she expected a backlash of some sort.

'That's great news, where are you moving to?' asked Kell.

'He lives in Hampstead, not far from the Heath,' replied Luci.

'Very nice,' he turned to Molly. 'And where are you going to live then?' He tried to keep his voice serious but couldn't help breaking into a big smile and giving his girlfriend a questioning look.

*

When Kell walked into his favourite Indian restaurant at the bottom of Monument Street, he was surprised to see that his friend was waiting for him at a table by the window. He checked his watch and saw he was pretty much on time so for the first time ever DCI Chris Packham was early.

They engaged in a clumsy man hug before sitting down in front of a couple of pints of Kingfisher.

'I assumed old habits remain and that you'd appreciate a pint of ice-cold lager,' said Packham.

'Cheers,' replied Kell before taking a couple of large swigs.

It was twelve months since they'd seen each other when Kell had helped on the Mandara case up in Manchester, so they had plenty to catch up on as they worked their way through the poppadoms and starters. When they'd exhausted the work discussions, Packham asked, 'So how's everything with you and Molly?'

'Great, in fact, better than great. She'd moving into my flat in a couple of weeks.'

Kell explained how Molly's flatmate was moving out and that it just felt the natural thing to do.

'Isn't your place a bit small? Aren't you going to find something a bit bigger?'

'Probably but remember how much trouble that caused when Amy and I were looking for somewhere. We'll take it slow and see how things go,' replied Kell.

Packham took a deep breath and Kell sensed the main reason for the meeting was about to be revealed.

'Actually, it's Molly that I want to talk about,' said Packham.

Kell didn't say anything, just gave his friend a perplexed look.

'I'm moving back to London to set up a bespoke cyber-crime and fraud team. It's the fastest growing area the serious criminals are getting involved with and there's a political will to show the government is doing everything it can to combat it.'

'It's great you're back down here, Chris, but what has this got to do with Molly?'

'I'd like to offer her a job. She did brilliantly on the Mandara case and she's got the background and experience that we're looking for.'

'Oh, I see,' was all Kell could manage.

'Of course, if you don't want me to, that's absolutely fine. I don't want to cause any friction between the two of you, especially as it's all going so well.'

'OK, well, er, I probably need to think about it. Well, er, actually, I don't as it's nothing to do with me. It's Molly's decision. What would she be doing?' replied a flustered Kell as he processed what his friend was asking.

'It's all office based, so there's no personal risk. A lot of it is tracking the source of funds from either Organised Crime Groups or persons of interest. Finding the origin, linking it to specific crimes and activities which we can use to build a case. We also know that a number of our banks, here in the city turn a blind eye to money laundering as they don't want to upset their wealthy clients,' he paused and looked at his friend who was closely following everything he said.

'The pay's good and there's opportunities for advancement.'

'And when would she start, assuming she says yes?' asked Kell.

'As soon as possible, so I guess that's as soon as you can find a replacement for her,' replied Packham.

'Funnily enough, we've been advertising for a third member of the team as the workload has increased so much. I'm sitting on a load of CVs although we haven't started to vet them yet.'

Having gotten over the initial shock of his friend's request, Kell began to realise it maybe wasn't such a bad idea if Molly did decide to work for the Met. It would certainly separate their personal and working lives and might actually help the relationship if they weren't together twenty-four hours a day.

'OK, it sounds like a great opportunity. Can you come to the office first thing in the morning to talk it through with her?' asked Kell.

'Sure, is 9 o'clock, OK?'

'Perfect, now let's have one for the road,' said Kell as he tried to catch the waiter's eye.

When the intercom buzzed just after nine the following morning, Molly was on the phone with a client, so Kell checked it was his friend and let him in. Packham walked into the office just as Molly was finishing her call.

'Chris, what are you doing here?' she cried.

'He's come to see you,' interjected Kell, before Packham could answer. 'I'll go and get some coffees from Costa, whilst Chris gives you the heads up.'

Kell took his time and got back to the office twenty minutes later with two Americanos and a peppermint tea for Molly. When he walked in, he heard Molly say, 'And when would I start?'

'It's all agreed then, is it?' said a smiling Kell as he handed them their drinks.

'No, it's not all agreed,' replied Molly. 'Not until we've discussed it properly.' She paused, 'But it is very exciting.'

'Right, I've got to get back to the Yard. If you could let me know by the end of the week Molly, that'd be great.'

Once Packham had left, Kell walked around the table and took his girlfriend in his arms.

'Well,' he said, 'what do you think?'

'I think it's a great opportunity and very exciting, but we need to discuss it properly. We've a lot going on here at the moment and then there's the fact we're moving in together, so it's not just about me. It's about us. So let's talk through everything this evening and once we've slept on it, I'll let Chris know what our decision is.'

5

The discussion that evening didn't take long. Molly made sure they considered how her moving to the Met would affect all aspects of their lives and it quickly became clear that the only stumbling block was the current workload that had seen them turning away good business in last couple of months.

'I think we should prioritise the recruitment alongside trying to clear the backlog of outstanding cases. If we can find somebody who has a short notice period or is looking for a first job after leaving Uni, then they should be able to start in a few weeks,' said Molly.

'Makes, sense. How many do you think we should take on? We were planning to take on an extra pair of hands before Chris tempted you away,' replied Kell.

'The workload certainly means we need two more people, but it's the training of them, that's going to be the problem.'

'You didn't need much training. In fact, you ended up training me some of the time!' Kell laughed and pulled out a stack of CVs he'd put into his backpack. 'We've got some good quality candidates here.'

Molly picked them up and started to sift through them. 'There's a mix of experienced ex-copper types and people like me looking to get into the industry. It might work if we looked for one of each. Someone who could hit the ground running and quickly start billing clients and a graduate who could start on the admin like I did.'

'Sounds like a plan. Let's go in early in the morning and work up a short list we can send to the agency to set up some interviews. And I think you should tell Chris you can start at the beginning of September. That gives us six weeks to get at least one person started. Now, do you fancy some reheated vegetable lasagne? I'm starving.'

'You certainly know how to impress a girl and does it go with an early night if we're getting up early in the morning?' Molly smiled as she walked into the small kitchen.

'I think I could manage that,' replied Kell. 'You sure, I don't want to wear you out.'

Kell laughed and sat there thinking he couldn't remember a time when he'd been happier.

*

'Justin Kell's office, Molly speaking, how may I help you?'

Molly listened intently to the caller who was clearly in some distress. Eventually, she was able to interject.

'I'm really sorry but as I mentioned yesterday when you rang, Mr Kell isn't taking on any new cases at the moment.'

The caller was persistent and wouldn't let Molly conclude the conversation. Eventually, she managed, 'Mr Kell is on the other line at the moment and he will only tell you the same as I have, that we're not currently taking on new clients.'

Kell, who wasn't on the phone gave his assistant a quizzical, *What's going on look.*

Molly politely put the caller on hold and referred to her scribbled notes.

'It's a Miss Zornitsa Elianti, this is the third time she's called. Her partner has gone missing and she says the police aren't taking his disappearance seriously. She wants you to take the case. She sounds desperate and is pleading that we listen to her.'

'It's not often that we get someone who sounds this desperate. What are the circumstances?'

'She got a WhatsApp from him last week, saying he was taking a break from work and going away for a few days to clear his head. She hasn't heard from him since and his phone just goes straight to voicemail. She's almost hysterical, convinced something bad has happened to him.'

Kell thought for a moment, 'Ask her to come in this evening at six thirty. Let's hear the full story before making a decision.'

Molly nodded in agreement as she reconnected the call, inviting an extremely grateful Miss Elianti to the office that evening.

Going through the CVs took longer than they had expected and they kept returning to it throughout the day. Finally, they managed to produce a short list of eight just before the outer door buzzer rang just before six-thirty.

'Good timing,' said Kell. 'Could you get the names across to the agency and ask them to set up the interviews as soon as possible. I'll go and let our potential client in.'

Kell decided he'd walk down to greet Zornitsa Elianti instead of simply buzzing her in. He felt that initial first impression was important, especially in a case like this.

'Miss Elianti, I'm Justin Kell, pleased to meet you.'

He held out his hand for the formal greeting only for the woman to throw her arms around his neck and break into floods of tears. He did his best to calm her down as he led her up to the office where Molly was seated at the meeting table.

'I'm so sorry, I'm in such a state, but I haven't slept properly for days. I'm just so relieved that finally, someone will listen to me.'

'Come and sit down and tell us everything from the beginning,' Kell gestured for her to take a seat next to Molly.

'What would you like to drink, Miss Elianti?' asked Molly.

'Coffee, please. Strong and black and please call me Zorna.'

When they were settled with their drinks, Kell nodded to Molly to take the lead.

'Right, let's start with all the basic details, name, address, email, mobile number, work details.'

Zorna ran through the information in a monotone. She was thirty-one years old and lived just outside Slough with her partner. They were currently renting, saving up to buy their first home. She worked for an upmarket estate agency in the West End and enjoyed her job. By the time they'd gone through the routine stuff, she had calmed down and both Kell and Molly saw a young woman who was just about holding it together.

'Thanks for that, Zorna. Now, please can you run through your partner's details.'

'His name is Emile Black and he used to work for Streem Bank.'

'And when was the last time you saw Emile?'

'It was last Friday. He's been having all sorts of problems at work. He was concerned about some of the things they were asking him to do and had a couple of differences of opinion with his boss. He went in early that Friday, planning to resign. I do a half day on Friday so we'd arranged to meet for lunch, but I got a WhatsApp from him late morning saying he'd handed in his notice and needed time to clear his head and was going away for a few days. I still hoped he might show up for lunch but when he didn't, I called and texted him all afternoon but didn't get a reply. Still haven't had a reply.'

'Could you show me the WhatsApp, please,' asked Kell.

Zorna got out her phone and scrolled through to the WhatsApp and handed Kell her phone.

'Does this sound like Emile? Is there anything unusual about it?'

He handed the phone to Molly.

'Well, it's quite abrupt. I don't know how to describe it,' said Zorna.

'He hasn't signed off with any kisses or emojis,' said Molly. 'Is that unusual?'

'Yes, it is. He always puts loads of hearts and stuff at the end. I put it down to him feeling stressed and not being himself. That's not unusual, is It?'

'Probably not,' said Kell, not wanting to worry here any further. 'Have you spoken to anyone at the bank?'

'Yes, I rang them and spoke to the HR Director. She said that she'd met with Emile that morning and accepted his resignation. They agreed to pay him for part of his notice period and they'd parted on amicable terms. She said he left the office about 11 o'clock which was about the time he sent the WhatsApp.'

'And what about the police?'

'Like you, they took all the details, but basically, as he's a thirty-four-year-old man and in their mind, there's nothing suspicious about his disappearance, they said they'd make some enquiries, but I reckon they think he's just left me.' This prompted another bout of tears and they waited until she'd calmed down before continuing.

'Right,' said Kell. 'We'll take the case. We'll start first thing in the morning. We need you to sign our terms of business which includes the payment of an upfront fee. Molly will take you through this now and I'll type up what we've discussed and open a case file. I'm sure we'll get to the bottom of this Zorna. There's usually a simple explanation in matters like this.'

He hoped his confident, matter-of-fact manner, didn't show the worry he was really feeling.

The look that Molly gave him, showed she had the same concerns.

6

Saul's good mood following his interview at Streem was maintained throughout the evening when his system of splitting his chosen numbers and the placing of variable stakes according to his cash level consistently delivered decent returns.

When he was at university, he'd taken a module on statistical modelling and probability. One of the first probability concepts he'd read about was tossing a coin and predicting if it would come down as a head or a tail. Both results were equally likely so it was simply chance as to what you called. If you tossed the coin 100 times, then each time it remained a 50/50 chance irrespective of what the previous result had been.

At this point, his gambling career was in its infancy and when he came across the grains of rice on a chess board analogy, the foundation of his various systems of playing roulette was formed. Quite simply, if you put a grain of rice on the corner square of a chess board and tossed a coin, then whatever you called had a 50/50 chance of being correct. If you lost, you had to put two grains on the next square.

By doubling, you're stake on the next toss you had a 50/50 chance of winning your grain of rice back plus a profit from the two you'd just staked. If you lost, then you doubled up to four grains on the next square and so on until you won. Saul quickly related this to roulette, red and black and replaced grains of rice with £1 roulette chips. If you consistently bet on "red" and doubled up your stake if you lost, then it would very likely only take a few spins for you to either win or get your money back. So in his mind, you couldn't lose.

Of course, to win big you needed an extended run of good luck, so he expanded his system to include single bets on individual numbers using the same principle that the probability was they'd come in at some point. All you needed was enough money to ensure you were still at the table when they did.

Variations included covering two or four numbers depending on how much available funds you had at the time. The unfortunate problem that Saul had was in the beginning he had won consistently and the buzz was better than anything he'd experienced in his entire life. But of course, it didn't last. When reading about the grains of rice on a chessboard, he dismissed the fundamental point that the author was making. There are 64 squares on a chess board and if you "lost" on just twenty consecutive occasions you'd need over a million grains of rice—

As it approached midnight, he was over a thousand pounds up and for once in his addicted life he decided to quit while he was ahead. The casino starts to get really busy from about 11.30 and he much preferred to play when there was only a couple of other people at the table. He cashed in his chips at the table but didn't bother going to the cashier, as he knew he would back early tomorrow evening.

He jumped in a taxi and as it headed through the still busy streets of the capital, he shut his eyes and replayed the events of the day.

The conversation with his brother was concerning. He knew Bill had his problems and whilst they weren't close, this was the first time he'd witnessed a defeated tone of abject misery. He'd sounded as though he was prepared to give up, but what would that look like? He wouldn't do anything stupid, would he? Anyway, there was little he could do before he went up to the family home a week on Sunday.

He woke early on the Saturday morning, feeling as though he'd been jolted awake from a bad dream. He couldn't remember what it was about, but he was sure that Bill was involved and something bad had happened. His mind drifted back to his earliest memories of them both as children.

With only twenty months between them, it had helped develop the bond they had with Bill always his hero. His big brother who looked out for him, helped him out when he got into all sorts of scrapes with the older boys at school or covered for him at home when he broke one of his parents many rules.

They didn't see much of their father. He was away on business a lot of the time and when he was at home he was always working in his office and seldom got involved in their childhood. He could only remember one family holiday they all went on together. He must have been ten and Bill twelve. They drove up to the West coast of Scotland and stayed in what seemed to a ten-year-old to be a castle but was in fact the country home of some laird that was a business associate of his father's.

There was a housekeeper who cooked all their meals and her husband who prepared the fires in the huge grates and worked on the grounds with the gardeners. Saul couldn't recall any happy memories from the holiday. He and Bill were left to their own devices and on the odd occasion when it wasn't raining, they explored the grounds, climbing trees and trying to catch tadpoles and newts in the various ponds.

As it turned out, the holiday was a watershed for the brothers. When they got back, Bill went off to boarding school and by the time Saul got there two academic years later, his brother didn't want to know his "first-year" sibling. The distance between them at school continued in the holidays when they returned home. They had different interests, different friends, different outlooks on life.

University saw them at different ends of the country. Saul studied maths at St Andrews whilst Bill got into Oxford, much to the delight of his mother, to study classics. Maybe Bill was the more academic, the dreamer, with Saul the pragmatic realist who was more prepared for the real world. In any event, they lived very different lives although the bond of blood kept them in touch and their relationship matured into one of mutual respect and the common interest of their inheritance.

At times, he wondered who was the more damaged. Bill sounded as though he was coming to the end of his tether and he clearly saw his brother as a source of comfort and help. Saul laughed out loud as this thought swept through his mind. He knew he had a gambling problem. It began when he was seventeen and started going into pubs and playing the fruit machines.

Once he started, he found he couldn't stop and after a while, his friends got bored of watching the endless spins and requests to borrow money. He didn't feel he was in any position to give advice to his brother.

Here he was on Saturday morning, the weekend ahead of him and all he had to do, all he wanted to do was go to the casino. It was pathetic. He sat up on the edge of the bed, put his head in his hands and cried for a long time.

Over the years he'd toyed with the idea of getting help with his addiction but had never taken the step to pick up the phone or go and see the doctor. That morning as he lay in bed he finally came to a decision. This week he'd ease back on his attendance at Rupert's, just go every other day. He'd go tonight and then have Sunday off.

He'd follow this routine throughout the week and when he met with Bill on Sunday, he'd talk to him about his problem and take the first steps to finally get the help he needed. Once he was satisfied that this was a plan he could stick to he got out of bed and started to fill his day, essentially just killing time until he headed west to begin stage one of his strategy to redemption.

As he sat on DLR on Monday morning, he considered how his latest plan to kick his habit had gone. On the positive side, he hadn't gone out on Sunday evening as per his every other day approach, but this was more than tempered by the fact that he'd quickly lost the £500 cash he'd taken on Saturday, plus another £400 which had seen him through to just after midnight before his luck or was it bad luck had ended his evening.

He got paid on Thursday, which on the plus side meant it would be three days without making a bet, but this meant he was already feeling what he could only describe as withdrawal symptoms, as his anxiety levels increased at the prospect.

He was at his desk at eight-thirty and scrolling through his emails when his mobile rang. He saw the caller ID and quickly answered.

'Hi, Markita.'

'Morning, Saul, how was weekend?'

'Not too bad, quite quiet really, how about you?'

'I spent most of it working, much to my husband's annoyance, but we did get out on Sunday afternoon for a nice long walk. Anyway, let's get straight to the point. The people at Streem were very impressed with you. Suzie, the HR director, rang me half an hour ago and asked if you could free up some time late afternoon to go and meet the rest of the board. She gave me lots of positive feedback and I think the job's yours if you want it.'

'Wow, they don't let the grass grow under their feet, I wasn't expecting to hear anything until later in the week,' replied Saul.

'They're a very dynamic firm and particularly liked your wanting to work somewhere more entrepreneurial. This however does create a minor problem. If the board like you, then they want you to start on 1 September. I know that's just six weeks away and your notice period is what? Six months?'

'Yeh, six months, but I'm sure I can negotiate. But six weeks is no time for them to find a replacement for me.'

'Let's take one step at a time. Can you get over there about four o'clock? They've a board meeting starting at five and should they want to appoint you, they can formally approve the appointment this evening.'

'Just let me check my diary,' replied Saul. He opened up his calendar and saw he had back-to-back staff reviews all afternoon. 'I can probably move a couple of staff meetings and get over there for four. It won't take more than an hour will it?'

'I don't think so, but it's best to be on the safe side, in case there's delays at their end,' replied Markita.

'OK, I'll be there at four o'clock,' said Saul.

'Great, ask for Suzie Canning, you met her on Friday. Good luck and give me a call as soon as you've finished.'

'Will do and thanks, Markita.'

The call ended and Saul sat at his desk smiling and nodding as he thought through the implications of a new job with a bigger salary and bonuses. All thoughts of his step-by-step approach to reducing his gambling problems temporarily forgotten.

He quickly rearranged his staff reviews and cleared his diary from three thirty. One of his more diligent staff always stayed well into the evening, so he moved her review to six fifteen. That way it didn't look like he'd just decided to finish mid-afternoon resulting in questions being asked.

He arrived at Steam at 3:55 and a couple of minutes later a smiling Suzie Canning emerged from the elevator to greet him.

'Good to see you again, Saul.' They exchanged the usual pleasantries as the lift took them to the fifth floor, where there was another reception desk and several large meeting rooms.

'Not all of the board members are here yet, but we'll get started straight away. They're waiting for you in the main boardroom.'

She led him into a large room which was similar in size and layout to the various ones he'd been in over the years. He was shown to the seat at the head of the long oval table and counted six people, four men and two women staring intently at him. He gave them a nervous smile and nod of the head, as Canning made the introductions.

He noticed the CEO wasn't present as one by one they went around the table asking him questions. After ten minutes, two more people slipped into the room and took their seats. A man and a woman who were very casually dressed and didn't have the usual stack of papers or a tablet with them. They didn't ask any questions and Suzie Canning didn't introduce them as she had done the others.

Twenty-five minutes later, it was done. No difficult questions and as he got more relaxed, he felt very comfortable as Canning asked him to wait outside in the reception area.

Once, the door was shut, she addressed the room, 'Well, any questions or objections?'

There were nods of approval and "nothing from me", "seems like he'll fit in well". Suzie looked at the couple sitting at the far end of the table who had come in late.

It was the woman who spoke, 'Time is off the essence. We must move quickly on Operation Waterloo. If Mr Solomons can help us achieve this, then you have our full support.'

The man sitting next to her nodded.

'Very well, I'll take him to meet Abebe and offer him the job,' said Canning.

Saul was pacing around the reception area sipping a bottle of water when Suzie Canning, emerged from the boardroom.

'Just one more meeting, Saul. Follow me please.'

They went down to the main office area and he followed her into the CEO's office where Abebe Bah sat behind his desk. They shook hands and took the two seats opposite him.

It was Bah who spoke first, 'Congratulations Saul, we'd like to offer you the job. Suzie will deal with salary, bonus, T and Cs etc, but the critical thing is that you must start working for us immediately.'

'Immediately? Er, I can't start immediately. I have a notice period. Markita said it, could be 1 September.'

Bah nodded to his HR Director.

Canning took the lead, 'Your official start date will be the 1 September, but there is a project we want you to work on unofficially with immediate effect. Something that you are in the perfect position to help us with. If you are successful, we will pay you an initial bonus as a welcome to the business.'

'And what is the project?' asked a perplexed Saul.

Bah leant forward and looked him straight in the eye. 'We want to buy the Wellington School where your brother works and we want him to run it.'

*

Abebe Bah was born in The Gambia on 25 May 1977. A bright child he thrived at school and was top of his class in many subjects. His father was a middle-ranking official in the government in Banjul, with his mother staying at home to look after him and his younger sister.

Abebe was academic, a very smart kid, working hard to achieve his dream of leaving Gambia and studying in the UK. His dedication paid off and being the outstanding student at his college, he gained a scholarship to Aston University to study Business and Finance, which he accepted, turning down an unconditional offer from the University of The Gambia.

As he sat back in his office reflecting on his first impressions of Saul Solomons, his mind drifted back to that decision he made in 1995 to leave his family and friends in his native country and go to England to continue his studies. That was the start of the long road that led him to where he was today. The twenty odd years since then had justified the tears of his mother and sister when he told them he was going. His stoical father simply nodding his acceptance of the decision.

As well as being committed to his studies, he knew he'd need money to support the modest scholarship. He'd never been afraid of hard work but quickly realised that working in bars late at night and at the weekend didn't earn him the cash he needed. When he returned home after his first year at Aston a chance meeting with a friend of his father gave him his first opportunity of working for himself.

As a predominantly import country, the businessmen and women of The Gambia were always looking for the cheapest possible commodities from around the world. This was the case with a big demand for second-hand tyres for cars, busses and lorries. There were no quality or safety standards as such and an unreliable supply chain from China presented a clear and lucrative opportunity.

In his first year in England, he'd noticed various sites around Birmingham where there were huge piles of second-hand tyres that he later discovered would end up being burned or sent to landfill. His father obtained the required paperwork and when he returned to the UK in early September he set about filling containers with second-hand tyres and sending them to his homeland.

He continued with this throughout his five years at Aston, extending his studies to obtain an accountancy qualification. When he had enough money, he started buying up small pieces of land outside of Banjul, foreseeing that as the economy continued to grow, so would the need for land around the capital. He was an entrepreneur and his next venture saw him setting up a money transfer business for people like him in the UK to send money to their families back in The Gambia.

Unlike now, there was limited regulation of such activity, so with his friend Francis Hall, they established a business that was still thriving twenty years later.

He paused in his reverie as he thought of Francis. Francis was a crook, even way back then. Now, like himself, he was full-blown criminal of the worst kind.

Deciding his academic life had run its course and having attained his British citizenship, he returned to Africa to begin his career. His father's connections got him a job in neighbouring Senegal in the foreign office where he quickly moved up the ranks but more importantly started to make the political and commercial connections that would help his ambition to revolutionise the banking sector in West Africa.

Despite his strict upbringing, Abebe was not concerned about breaking a few rules to get what he wanted. He witnessed it all the time and understood that who you knew was as important as what you knew. He moved from the foreign office to the National bank in Senegal and so began his meteoric rise in the banking industry in West Africa.

Technology, security and reputation were the simple foundations of how he transformed an unreliable and corrupt industry into one fit for the 21st century. There was of course one big problem. The criminals who used the banks to run their operations and launder their money weren't happy. They were being forced out of arrangements and backhanders that had gone on for years, with Abebe Bah the focus of their rage.

So being pragmatic and seeing the opportunity to make even more money, he struck a deal. Subject to certain conditions, the cartel of banks using the new systems and technology he'd introduced would continue to facilitate the movement of the various foreign currencies for the most powerful of the crime lords. The smaller players would be frozen out or taken over by the larger gangs and Bah would receive a personal cut of each transaction.

To ensure the smooth operation of moving large sums of money through the system, he called on the services of his old friend Francis Hall, whose expertise in such matters had been proven in the Far East. Together they became the perfect team. The outgoing, charming, suave and sophisticated Bah became the public face of everything they did. Hall did not like people.

He did not like engaging with anyone unless he absolutely had to. He only spoke when he had to and even with Bah, he was often monosyllabic. But it worked and now here they were in London about to set up their biggest operation yet.

7

Apart from his friend Chris Packham, Kell still had a few contacts in the Met who were happy to share information in appropriate circumstances, so when he rang the morning after their meeting with Zornitsa Elianti, it didn't take him long for him to get put through to the officer in charge of the case.

The methodology for such cases is fairly standard and the officer ran through what was a textbook approach in the circumstances. Emile Black had been reported missing last Friday by his girlfriend. There were no suspicious circumstances and they'd confirmed with the bank that Emile had gone to see the HR Director, a Ms Suzanne Canning, that morning and handed in his resignation. This was accepted, as there had been some performance issues recently and they'd agreed to pay him for two months of his notice period. They parted on amicable terms and that was that.

'Did they elaborate on the performance issues?' asked Kell. 'No and we didn't press the point.'

'What about the phone that sent the WhatsApp to Zorna? Was it a work phone or a personal one?' asked Kell.

'It was his own phone, he did have a work mobile which he handed back on the Friday, together with a tablet.'

'Have you tried to locate where the phone is now?'

Kell could sense the officer's irritation building when he replied, 'Of course, we have, Mr Kell. The phone must be switched off and certainly hasn't been used since Friday. This would appear consistent with someone who doesn't want to be contacted. And before you ask, we've also got markers on his bank cards, which will flag when and where they are used.'

'Thanks. That's all I need for now. Will you keep me posted if there are developments?'

'Certainly, Mr Kell. Goodbye.'

'How did that go?' asked Molly from the other side of the office.

'They've done everything you'd expect. It's clear the police think he's simply walked away from the relationship. If that is the case, then he'll have to use his bank cards soon, as you can't survive without money.'

'And what do you think?' asked Molly.

'I think you're going to go to Streem and see what you can find out.'

They decided that Molly wouldn't phone ahead and try to arrange an appointment. Most organisations, especially banks being very good at stonewalling and blocking access to key personnel. If Molly turned up and refused to leave until she saw Ms Canning or someone in authority, then there was a better chance of moving the case on quickly.

She arrived at the office in Farringdon just after 11.00 AM and asked the receptionist if she could see Suzie Canning.

'Do you have an appointment?'

'No, but it's very important that I see her,' replied Molly.

'I'm afraid, Ms Canning doesn't see anyone without an appointment. I can make one now for you if you can tell me what it's about.'

Molly got a business card from her purse and handed it to the receptionist.

'I'm Molly Cribbs from Justin Kell's office. We're a private investigation firm and I'd like to talk to Ms Canning about Emile Black.' Very polite and professional, Molly watched intently for any reaction at the mention of Black's name.

The receptionist studied the card intently before looking up. 'I think I've heard of Justin Kell, he's been in the news recently, hasn't he? Oh my god! You're not the woman who was kidnapped and tortured in that cellar are you?'

A look of incredulity spread across her face.

Molly was still having counselling in the aftermath of the ordeal. Initially, she thought she could cope by simply being with Justin, but then the flashbacks started when she had these brief moments of uncontrollable terror. Her counsellor's view was the more she talked about her time in Jimmy Skaa's cellar the more she'd be able to cope with the memories that were usually triggered by people either referring to it directly or finding herself in a confined space.

There were two scenarios that kept repeating themselves. The first was the moment she met Skaa outside of Leytonstone Underground station and the second was the witnessing the horrific murder of Gary Jones. One this occasion it was the moment she first met the madman.

'Excuse me, Miss, would you be a Molly Cribbs?' At the same time, he flashed his old warrant card and put a serious frown on his face.

'Er yes, yes, I am. What's the matter, have I done something wrong.'

'Not at all. It's Justin Kell, he's in a bit of bother and we need you to come to the scene.'

Her mind takes her to being pushed down a blurred street by Skaa, moving faster and faster as her panic increases.

They were now walking briskly through a rundown area and there was nobody on the streets except them.

'Do you have any idea who this man may be, Molly? He's asking for you by name?'

'Er yes, his name is Skaa and he's a madman.'

Pure terror as she realises that something is terribly wrong. She can physically feel her arm being squeezed as he pushes her down the street. She tries to pull her arm free from his grip, but he just squeezes tighter and increases their pace.

She's struggling to break free but then he punches her and breaks her nose, which she subconsciously touches her as she hears the crack of it breaking in her mind.

Molly wasn't unconscious but she was dazed. A feeling of pure terror ran through her as he pushed her down some steps into a dark room. When her head hit the stone floor, she slipped into the relief of unconsciousness.

The noise of her head hitting the stone floor, snaps her back to the present. In real-time, the ordeal had lasted just over five minutes, in flashback it was five seconds.

'Yes, that's me,' replied Molly calmly.

The receptionist gave her a curious look, 'Just a moment, please.'

The receptionist got up and went to a door next to the lifts, put her name tag card against the reader and went through to what Molly assumed must be the main office.

Interesting, she thought, *that she hadn't just rung through to speak to the HR Director.* Very interesting indeed.

Five minutes later she reappeared and gestured Molly over to the lifts. The door opened and she ushered Molly in and pressed the button for the third floor.

'Ms Canning will be waiting for you,' she said, leaving Molly alone in the lift.

Molly smiled as the lift doors closed, desperately concentrating on the job she was here to do and praying she didn't have another flashback to the ordeal she'd been through in that basement.

Also smiling was Suzie Canning, as the lift doors opened Molly was greeted by the HR Director.

'Miss Cribbs, I'm Suzie Canning, pleased to meet you.'

'Please, call me Molly and thanks for seeing me without an appointment.'

She led Molly to a small meeting room, closing the door as they entered.

'I must admit, I'm intrigued as to why you want to see me. I understand from Judi, that you and Mr Kell are quite famous.'

'Not really, a case we were involved with made the national news last year. I'm surprised anyone remembers it.'

'Judi, mentioned you wanted to talk about Emile?'

'Yes, his girlfriend reported him missing last Friday and we're working with the Met on the case.'

She watched for any change in the body language of the woman sitting opposite her and noticed she started tapping her pen on the desk.

'Missing, I wasn't aware that Emile was missing. I saw him last Friday when he handed his notice in.'

'At this stage, we believe you're the last person who saw him that day. How did he seem when you were with him?'

'I'll admit it wasn't an easy meeting. He was insistent on resigning, whereas I was trying to talk him out of it.'

'Why did he want to resign?' asked Molly.

'I can't say too much because of the confidentiality agreement we signed,' she paused as if thinking what to say next. 'Let's just say there were personality clashes with some of the directors and his team.'

She hesitated when Molly didn't respond, the awkward silence stretching for an uncomfortable number of seconds. Eventually, Canning tried to change tack.

'So did the police ask you to get involved, I've already given them a statement and they seemed quite happy.'

'We've been retained by Emile's girlfriend. We'll be able to give a lot more time than the police would to the case. There are hundreds of misper cases reported each week in London alone and as I'm sure you're aware, police resources are really stretched.'

'Well, I don't think I can add anything else. When Emile left, he appeared to be in good spirits. We agreed to pay him a proportion of his notice period which I don't think he was expecting. We parted on good terms. Now if that's all Molly, I have a meeting to get to.'

As she stood to leave, Molly flicked through her notepad, checking off the questions she'd prepared. 'Just one more thing. Is there a staff entrance?'

'Er, no. Everyone comes and goes through the main reception area. Why do you ask?'

'I'd like to view the CCTV footage from last Friday to confirm the time Emile left the building. That way we should be able to track his movements and get an idea of where he went after your meeting.'

Following a moment's hesitation, Canning responded, 'I think that's handled by the security company for the building, I'll email you their details later this afternoon.'

All smiles, Molly replied, 'I'm happy to wait if you could ask someone to get them for me now. Every minute counts in investigations like this.'

'Of course, I'll get on to it straight away.'

When Canning had left, Molly got out her phone and started searching for the details of the office block that Streem was based in, including the security company. There were only a small number of providers of CCTV systems as they had to be vetted by the local authorities and linked into the police coverage across the city. The one used by the bank was a smaller operator who had recently come into the market. She was just noting the details when a smart-looking young man, probably a similar age to herself, came in and handed her a sheet of paper.

'Hi, I'm Mo. I understand you want the details of the security company for the building.'

'Thanks, Mo, yes.'

She studied the brief details which confirmed what she already knew but also had the contact details of the individual liaison officer for the bank.

'Are you involved with the security company?' asked Molly.

'No, I work in Ops, but my remit includes being the point of contact for the physical security of the building. Now, if that's everything I must get back to work.'

He opened the door and escorted Molly to the lift and went down with her to the ground floor where he tapped her through the turnstiles with his pass.

It was a thirty-minute walk back to the office on Brick Lane and Molly had a smile on her face the whole way. She was sure Justin would be impressed with her morning's sleuthing.

8

Saul looked at the CEO opened-mouthed, trying to compute what he'd just heard.

'You want to buy the Wellington School and you want to appoint Bill as the Principal?' he replied very slowly.

'Yes, he will in effect be working for us,' replied Bah. 'Er and why do you want to buy Wellington?'

'A key part of our strategy is for the bank to invest in businesses that aren't performing as well as they might. We have several of our wealthy clients who see the private education sector as having real potential. The purchase would in effect be by a consortium of which the bank would have a stake. We have completed a certain level of due diligence on a number of similar institutions and intend to make an initial offer to purchase Wellington by the end of this week.'

Bah's tone was so convincing that Saul was lost for words.

Canning interjected on a nod from the CEO. 'And before you ask, the job offer we are making, has nothing to do with your relationship with your brother. If you decide to turn us down, we will still proceed with the Wellington deal.'

Saul was nodding his head, deep in thought. Finally, he said, 'But why Bill? He's really struggling at the moment and is considering whether he should leave. Also, he doesn't have any experience of being a headteacher let alone Principal.'

Bah replied, 'Our due diligence has determined that the current incumbent, Mark Smith, is not up to the job and does not have the profile we're looking for. The rest of the senior leadership team are adequate, but we will leave it to your brother to decide who stays and who goes. Of the current team, he is by far the best candidate and we don't have time to go to the market as we want to complete the deal next month, before the start of term in September.'

'But I don't see where I fit in. If the deal is nearly done, what difference can I make?'

It was Canning who responded. 'We need you to convince your brother to take the job. The whole deal depends on it.'

'And,' said Bah, 'there is a lot at stake.'

Saul asked the one question that had been spinning around in his mind, 'You mentioned an initial bonus if this all works out. How much would that be?'

'There are various regulatory matters that need attending to, in a deal such as this, so you will need to undertake these as well. Subject to completion in August, then it will be a six-figure sum. I assume we have your acceptance to these terms?' asked Bah, who stood up and offered his hand.

'I'm in,' replied a beaming Saul. The handshake confirming his fate.

'The team working on the deal are meeting at six this evening and it is important you attend. It will likely be close to midnight before it finishes, so please cancel any arrangements you may have. Once you've done that, Suzie will have your contract ready and will go through everything from an HR perspective. You will hand your resignation in tomorrow morning. For the rest of this week, the deal team will meet every evening and you will attend. Suzie will show you to your new office.'

Another handshake and he was dismissed.

His "new" office was just down the corridor, in between the FDs and Cannings.

'Here you are,' she said. 'I'll be back in half an hour to go through the paperwork. You've a lot to take in and I'm sure you'll have plenty of questions for me. But in the meantime, please ensure your diary is free to accommodate what Abebe just ran through.'

She left, leaving him gazing around his office which was slightly bigger but better furnished than his current one. He sat at his desk taking in the bizarre events of earlier. For once, he wasn't distracted by thoughts of gambling and getting to the casino. It was as though his brain had been shocked out of its rhythm and was now programmed to a different frequency. He wasn't sure how he felt about that, but for the time being, he felt good, as he began to comprehend such a positive shift in this life.

He rang his PA and asked her to cancel the staff review he had scheduled for later and to clear his diary of any late meetings going forward. He was relieved when she said the boss was in all of the following day and arranged a meeting at nine in the morning. With that sorted, his thoughts turned to Bill and their get-together on Sunday.

His reverie was disturbed when Canning came in with the details of the job offer.

The financial package including the bonus scheme was incredible, way more than he was expecting. He signed everything that was put in front of him, without reading all the details and was then ushered down to the conference room for the first meeting of Operation Waterloo.

He wasn't surprised to see the man and woman from the board meeting sitting around the table with half a dozen others. For his benefit, they went around the table introducing themselves and their roles. The woman introduced herself as Bernice Schmidt, a German financier and the man, Dirk Paton, an American, no further comment provided.

As Bah had indicated the meeting went on until ten thirty when everyone seemed happy that sufficient progress had been made and key next steps agreed. Saul did not contribute anything, just sitting there taking everything in. The deal was basically straight-forward. The consortium of investors had made an initial offer to the shareholders of the school which had been turned down, despite what Saul thought were attractive terms.

A further offer had been agreed which as far as Saul could make out valued the school at £12m, which was a lot for an enterprise that was clearly losing money. The rationale in the prospectus was that with the right management team and investment the school had the potential to increase student numbers, increase the fee base and deliver significant profit.

There was no end-of-meeting chit-chat. The lateness of the hour meant that everyone headed straight home for a few hours' sleep before repeating the process the next day. Saul debated going to the casino but decided against it. He wouldn't be able to concentrate with everything that was spinning around in his head and he wanted time to think about the conversation with his boss in the morning. As he headed to Bank to get the DLR he couldn't keep the smile off his face.

The meeting with Adrian Collins the following morning went a lot better than he expected. Despite being what Saul regarded as a "conservative" banker, Collins was progressive with his views on staff promotions and advancement.

'I can't say that I'm not disappointed Saul, but I knew this day would come sooner or later. I'll not stand in your way despite the short notice period you want to work. It's a good move for you at this stage of your career. All I ask is that you maintain 100% commitment until you leave.'

'Of course, goes without saying. I was thinking it'd make sense to make an interim appointment in the short term, whilst you look for a permanent replacement. I know a few people who would be good if they're available.'

'Makes sense. If you could give the names to HR, they can start the processes.'

Collins stood up and held out his hand which Saul shook warmly.

'Thanks for being so open with me Saul and good luck at Streem.' And with that, the meeting was over.

For the rest of the week, Saul had never worked so hard in his life. He was basically working fourteen-hour days and by Friday evening he was exhausted as he made his way to Streem's office in Farringdon. He was early for the six-thirty meeting so went straight to his office to go through any emails that had come in that day relating to Operation Waterloo. Before his tablet had loaded, Canning and Bah walked in and sat down at the meeting table.

'Saul, glad you're early, there's a couple of things we need to go through with you,' said Bah.

Straight to the point, as usual, thought Saul.

'Earlier today, we made a further offer to the shareholders of the Wellington. The corporate finance team they've appointed has indicated that it is likely to be accepted when the Board meets on Monday. On this basis, we'd like you to meet with your brother this weekend and convince him to accept the job when we offer it to him, which will hopefully be sometime next week.'

Canning interjected, 'You told us you were seeing him this Sunday, but we suggest you go up there this evening as there is a lot for you to go through.'

Bah nodded and pushed what looked like a copy of the prospectus across the table. 'This is an internal document which details our plans for the school and how we intend to grow the revenue and profitability. It is highly confidential and must not leave your possession. You can show it to Bill, but he cannot have a copy at this stage.'

'Any questions?' asked Canning.

'Er, no, I don't think so,' replied a slightly mystified Saul.

*

Suzie Canning stood nervously in front of her boss's desk as he stared intently at the screen of his tablet. When he looked up, all he said was, 'Well?'

'We didn't anticipate a PI being brought into the case. It's also a concern that it's Justin Kell. You will see he has quite a reputation and a strong connection with the Met.'

'I didn't ask you to state the bleeding obvious!' Bah slammed his fist on his desk. 'What are we doing about it!' he yelled.

'The security company will delete the footage from Friday saying it was a technical glitch. We just need to stay calm and ride it out. With no physical evidence, they'll have to drop the case eventually.'

Canning was finding it hard to keep her composure. She'd witnessed the temper of her boss on a number of occasions and it hadn't ended well for those who stood in his way.

'I hope your right Suzie because everything we've worked for is on the line here,' and with a flick of his head she was dismissed.

She hurried back to her office, shut the door, sat behind her desk, put her head in her hands and tried to get her breathing under control. She banged the table, 'Shit, shit, shit!'

Things were quickly getting out of control, first with Black and now with Justin bloody Kell and his sidekick sniffing around. Her instincts told her to get out, make a run for it and leave Abebe and the weirdo Hall to clear up the mess. But there was always the same but. The money. She'd already been well rewarded since going Streem just prior to the launch a few years ago and that would be insignificant according to her boss when the Project Waterloo came online. It was just too much to give up now.

It had been a real struggle since the breakup of her marriage. When her thug of a now ex-husband literally threw her out onto the Bristol streets where they'd set up home, after what was the last of their vicious rows, she'd had nowhere to go, no one to turn to. They'd married young, both just twenty-two and as soon as they came back from their honeymoon in Santorini, the fights had started. It was always stupid little things like what was for tea, why was she going out, who should do the cleaning.

But later it got more about his involvement in a car stealing racket, that operated through the garage where he worked as the senior mechanic. She didn't like his "associates" whom he'd bring back to their flat for late-night drinking sessions. He'd make fun of her and criticise her in their presence and when she gave as good as she got, he'd hit her. She got to the point where she'd hit him back, often with plate or a vase and then everything just escalated.

With no family, she spent a couple of weeks sofa surfing until she found a bedsit which she could just afford on her HR Manager's salary. To get as far away from him as possible she started to apply for jobs in London and was surprised but delighted when she got an interview for a new bank that was starting up in the City. She didn't quite have the experience they was looking for but the agency didn't see that as a problem.

It was her second interview when she met Bah. He was charming and instead of questions about her other roles he focussed on her private life and how she'd come to apply for the job. She felt so comfortable with him that she bared her soul and told him everything about her past and the troubled marriage, including the fact that she'd got into debt and had a couple of CCJs against her name, together with a caution from the Bristol police for assault.

She remembered how when she'd finished, he just smiled and said, 'We are a very dynamic and entrepreneurial business. We are not conventional and we sometimes have to cut corners and do things that some people might be uncomfortable with. But from what you've told me I think you'll fit in very well here. And that was that. The job was hers.'

From the day she moved to London and started with Streem, the "unconventional" aspects of job quickly became apparent. She realised now that the more she turned a blind eye and didn't question Bah or Hall, the more she was sucked into their nefarious world. But she also enjoyed it. Not just the high salary and promises of big bonuses, but the thrill of the edginess of the whole operation and the confidence she had that Bah would look after her.

Now though, after Emile Black, she realised she was just a pawn in his game and just like her ex-husband, if she didn't comply, then she'd get hurt and this time it might be fatal.

9

Saul started reading the "highly confidential" document on the way back to his flat to pick up the clothes and toiletries he'd need for the weekend. As he turned the pages, he could hardly believe the plans they had for the school over the next five years.

New buildings, complete refit of the science block and IT centre, an overhaul of the student accommodation, the investment amount was stunning. The objective of making Wellington one of the most prestigious and outstanding private schools in the country appeared very credible. The big issue of course was ensuring they drove up student numbers significantly and there was a detailed section on how this would be achieved, albeit with several optimistic assumptions.

As he drove around the M25 trying to imagine how his brother would react to the news about the school and his future involvement should he accept the offer from the purchasers, he was conscious that the "itch" was back and had been slowly getting stronger in the last few days.

His work commitments had meant he hadn't been to the casino all week and whilst the adrenaline of working two jobs had initially kept it at bay, the gambling demon had slowly edged its way back into to the forefront of his mind. Knowing he wouldn't be able to do anything about it until Sunday evening had the dual effect of calming him down one minute and then increasing his anxiety the next.

The heavy traffic finally got a bit lighter as he headed up the M11 and decided he'd ring Bill first and then his mother.

Bill sounded genuinely pleased that he was coming up a couple of days early and that they'd be able to spend some time together. He didn't give a specific reason as to the change of plan, only saying there was something he needed to talk through with his brother.

His mother sounded less enthusiastic as she had already eaten and she made the prospect of preparing supper for Saul akin to the miracle of God giving the Israelites manna from heaven.

The country lanes that wended their way to the house were very quiet as usual. He didn't pass another car but as he turned into the long driveway, he saw a few people walking down the lane about a hundred yards past the turning. He thought it strange that anyone would be out this way so late, as it was just about fully dark.

His mind quickly turned to the matters at hand as the car crunched up the gravel path. Lights were on in both parts of the house, but it was his brother who came out to greet him as he pulled to a stop in front of the family home.

They embraced warmly. Bill carried his overnight bag up to the main front door where their mother had appeared and courtesy kisses on each cheek were exchanged.

'How lovely to see you, Saul, I'm so glad you were able to come up early,' said Esther. 'Come, we've time for a drink before you have supper.'

Bill poured three glasses of Rioja from an already open bottle and they sat around the kitchen table, catching up with each other's news. The supper of salmon, couscous and asparagus was delicious and whilst it didn't quite go with the red wine, Saul enjoyed it not realising how hungry he was. As soon as he'd finished eating, his mother put his plate in the dishwasher and declared she was going to bed.

'You're in your room, of course,' she said as she left the kitchen, 'we'll talk properly in the morning.'

'Sounds ominous,' said Bill, trying hard not to laugh.

'Nothing unusual there,' replied Saul. 'Anyway, there's something I need to talk to you about, open another bottle and let's get settled in the lounge.'

They sat opposite each other across a large coffee table. Saul took a sip from his wine and leant forward with his arms resting on his knees.

'I've got a new job at a bank in the city, Streem it's called and I start officially on 1 September. I'm also helping them with a deal they're working on at the moment.'

'Congratulations,' said Bill. 'I assume you'll be earning even more money than you are now!'

'Yes, it's a good package, but the deal I'm helping them with affects you.'

He paused, with his brother looking confused.

'How so?'

'Streem are leading a consortium of investors that are buying Wellington. Your board is meeting on Monday when it is expected they will accept the offer. They want the deal to complete before the start of term in September.'

Bill stood up and paced around the room. 'Wow, so it's actually happening. I bet they'll want to get rid of that idiot Smith, but then it's a case of who they replace him with.'

Saul stood up. 'That person is you, they will be formally offering you the job once the deal has been signed and it's very important that you accept.'

'What! Me? You're joking. Ha bloody ha, you are joking. Well, it's not funny brother, this could affect my career.'

'This is no joke, Bill. I'm deadly serious. They want you to be the Principal of the Wellington.' Bill sat back down and stared at his brother. Eventually, he managed, 'Why me?'

'To be honest with you, that's what I thought!' Saul laughed and took a large swig of his wine. 'There are two main reasons. The first is continuity. They need someone who can hit the ground running and in the due diligence process, quickly realised that the current guy Smith, is as you say, an idiot. Of the rest of the Senior Leadership team, you stand out as the most suitable to take his place. So the second reason is that you are the best man for the job.'

'But I've no experience in running a school! I wouldn't know where to start!'

'You probably know more than you realise and anyway, there'll be bank people on the board to help with the financials and the like. The plan is that you focus solely on the academic side and help with attracting more pupils, particularly from overseas.'

Bill was still shaking his head in shock.

'The other thing to consider is that your salary will be doubled and generous bonuses subject to pupil numbers and financial performance. Quite simply, it's an offer you can't refuse.'

'Right, an offer I can't refuse,' repeated Bill.

They stayed up into the early hours as Saul initially had to convince Bill that he was being serious and then going through the details of the plans for the school, the continuity that was so important in achieving them and how Bill could pick and choose his senior team, deciding who stays and who goes.

When Bill had finally run out of questions, Saul said, 'There is one final thing. I've been asked to be the bank's liaison with the school going forward. I'll sit on the board representing the shareholders. My focus will be ensuring the growth projections are being met, alongside revenue, profitability etc. I won't be interfering in any of the academic stuff, the hiring and firing or anything like that. How does that sound.'

Bill was quiet for a moment as he played through the scenario in his mind. Finally, he said, 'I think I can live with that. It will be good to see more of you. Right, I'm off to bed, although I doubt I'll sleep much. My head is spinning! So, just to be clear, this is not a wind-up and I'm going to be the Principal of Wellington?'

'Correct. Not a wind-up, brother. This will change your life,' replied Saul.

'OK. Look I'm playing golf in the morning, so I'll leave you to bond with mother, but why don't you come up to the club about two and we can have some lunch, talk some more.'

'Sounds like a plan, see you then.'

Saul switched off the lights and made his way to the bedroom he'd slept in for a long as he could remember. He was surprised but delighted with his brother's reaction and was looking forward to reporting back to his new boss on Monday morning.

Despite these good feelings, he was very conscious that the "itch" was getting stronger. He decided he'd leave straight after lunch on Sunday and get a session in at the casino. It seemed a long time away which was probably why he couldn't get to sleep as he tossed and turned dreaming of the spinning wheel.

After breakfast, Esther insisted that they stroll around the garden, so she could inspect and Saul thought, *Show off the range of beautiful flowers and shrubs.* The conversation was casual and relaxed and when they returned to the kitchen for some homemade lemonade, Saul felt the time was right tell her of his new job and make a commitment that he was confident he could keep.

'Actually, mother, I've got some good news for you. I'm starting a new job at the beginning of September. It's in the same field, but with a fairly new bank. I've got a place on the board, so it's a good step up.'

'Congratulations, I'm very pleased for you.'

'Also, I'll be paying you back the money I owe you in full at the beginning of September. The project I invested in has turned out well and I'm just waiting on the money coming through.'

'I'm very pleased to hear it. You shouldn't be relying on handouts from your parents at your age.'

'I know, but it would help Bill and I if we could have access to some of father's money. It's better that we get some of it now instead of waiting another twenty years.'

He hadn't intended to bring this up, but he was sure it would be a topic of conversation when he met with his brother later.

'I'll say the same to you as I did to William. Your father made specific instructions in his will of how the money should be passed on when he died. It would be dishonourable of me not to respect his wishes. So please, don't bring the matter up again. It really is quite vulgar talking about such things.'

Bill was waiting for him on the outside terrace at the golf club. His three playing partners were sitting with him in the warm summer sunshine. He recognised the faces from the days when he was a junior member and he quickly settled into the conversation.

It wasn't long before they'd finished their drinks and Bill and Saul went into the bar to order some sandwiches for lunch. They sat on a table for two by a large window overlooking the 18th green and Bill got straight to the point.

'I've a couple of questions on the job but they can wait. What I wanted to talk to you about is father's money and mother's reluctance to let us have any of it. She's sitting on millions of pounds and my view is if she doesn't change her position and let us have what father promised, then we formally contest the will. There's still time to do this, I've checked with Crabtree.'

'I did bring up the matter with her this morning and she clearly has no intention of letting us have any of it any time soon. She feels strongly that she must observe father's wishes. I didn't mention the contesting issue, which would be a big step and probably mean she'd never speak to us again, but I'm sure you know all this anyway.'

'Yes, yes, but excluding the house, she's got close to twenty million, what with the share portfolio, the other properties and cash in the bank. What's she going to do with it all?'

'It's the principle of the whole thing she's stubborn about. She doesn't want to go against father's wishes. I don't see how we can do anything, unless of course—' Saul was trying to be the voice of reason but could see his brother was only getting more and more worked up. He tried changing tack.

'Anyway, with your new job you'll get a big pay rise, so money won't be a problem.'

'Money isn't the main problem. In short, I don't like teaching, I don't like the kids and I don't like not having the money required so I can decide how to live my life, working or not. So, I'll see how becoming the Principal changes things as I won't be teaching the brats and I'll also be able to decide who stays and who goes. I'll give it a year, but I'm deadly serious about getting what's rightfully ours. I'll contest the will and don't give a shit if she doesn't speak to me ever again.'

'OK, I understand. Let's get the school thing sorted then we can decide how best to convince her to change her mind. We'll be seeing a lot more of each other in the coming weeks and months, so we'll have the time to sort this out. Now, let's have another drink before heading back.'

The rest of the weekend was uneventful, the brothers talked about the prospects for the school and the growth plans the new owners had. Wellington already had a license for a thousand pupils although the enrolment for September was only half this. The plan was to potentially double the capacity to close to two thousand and that would be the primary objective for the next twelve months.

Saul left straight after lunch on Sunday. He was relieved that Bill had been so positive about taking over and had already emailed Bah and Canning giving them the good news. They both responded immediately, congratulating him on a job well done. He felt good as he drove down the M11 heading back to London.

In fact, the prospect of getting to scratch the itch made him euphoric. He would later reflect that maybe it was this euphoria that made him forget some of the disciplines and systems he used when he was playing roulette, that resulted in his worst ever night at the table. He lost big, very big.

*

Roddy, Max, Al and Con sat in their Common Room drinking tea and Red Bull. Roddy was holding forth as usual and he had the undivided attention of his three friends.

'So, now, we've checked out where he lives, all we need to do is to decide how best to execute our plan.'

'What about the old woman, I assume that's his mum?' said Al.

'That's a minor issue. There's always collateral damage in a war,' replied Roddy. 'What will be will be.'

10

'Well, how did it go?' asked Kell as soon Molly walked into the office. 'Get the kettle on and I'll tell you all about it. I think you'll be impressed.'

When they had their drinks, Molly recounted every detail of her visit to Streem. Kell listened intently without interrupting. When she'd finished, she could see him processing the details of what she'd told him.

'Excellent work, I don't think I'd have done anything differently. It's a pity you're leaving me!'

She leaned over the meeting table where they were sitting and kissed him gently on the lips.

'It's only work my darling, I'll never leave you, you know that don't you.'

'Yes, I know that. It just won't be the same around here, that's all. Now, back to business. I assume your next step is contacting the security company?'

'Actually, I emailed them on my walk back. If they don't get back to me this afternoon, I'll ring them first thing in the morning. I got the feeling I spooked Suzie Canning when I told her we were working with the police. There's definitely something strange going on, something she's not telling me.'

'Your instincts are one of the most important weapons that a PI has. Always trust them and follow them and you won't go far wrong. Once we get the security footage, it should be easy to find out where he went after he left the bank.'

The reply from the security company came in overnight and was at the top of her inbox when Molly logged onto her laptop the following morning. She read the short email twice before turning to Justin.

'The case of Emile Black just got even more interesting. The security company have advised that I'm welcome to go to their office in Whitechapel any time to view the footage for the Friday Emile went missing but say there was a glitch in the backup server which means the records for that day are incomplete.'

'I suppose they're not saying the times they've lost or should I say intentionally deleted?' replied Kell.

'No, but I'm sure it will be no surprise that we won't see Emile leaving the building,' said Molly.

'Before you go over there, run a full background on the company, the directors, everything. You said they were new to the market so it will help to know who financed the start-up and also any other customers they've got.' He paused before adding, 'And I'll come with you. This is starting to look a lot more serious than another missing person's case.'

It took Molly most of the morning to find out everything she could about Matrix Security Ltd.

She updated Kell on what she'd found over a sandwich and salad lunch they had at their desks.

'The business was incorporated three years ago, which coincided with the launch of Streem Bank. One of the directors is Abebe Bah, who as we know is also the CEO of Streem. I cannot find any other clients for them and the office they use in Whitechapel is owned by a subsidiary of Streem. So, basically, it's one big happy family.'

'Right, let's head over there now, but whatever we find, let's not arouse any concerns or suspicions. Let's take the "these things happen" tack and give the impression that we think it's just another misper case. I can then report back to the Met and see how they want to proceed.'

They spent less than an hour at Matrix Security. A very helpful young man showed them the footage of Emile Black going into the bank at just before 11.00 AM before going completely blank about five minutes later.

'It happens from time to time,' the technician said, unprompted. 'Can be a power surge or a split-second break in the signal and the cameras stop recording. We have to reboot the whole system which takes about an hour.'

'Did you do the reboot on this occasion?' asked Molly. 'Yes, I was the only one in on that shift.'

'And when did you get everything back online?' This time it was Kell who asked the question.

'Let me see.' He hit a few keys and the footage resumed. 'Twelve-seventeen.'

Kell didn't respond immediately, noticing how twitchy the young tech was getting.

'Is there another exit from the building? For service vehicles, garbage collection and the like?'

'Er yes, at the back of the block?'

'And is that covered by CCTV?' asked Kell.

'Er, I think so?' replied the now visibly stressed technician. Kell gave him a big smile and simply said, 'Well?'

'I don't think I can show you that. I've not got access to that part of the system.' The man was now sweating considerably, despite the cool, air-conditioned temperature within the building.

Kell took out his phone and started scrolling through his contacts. He tapped a number and put the phone to his ear but spoke to the now panic-stricken young man.

'We're working with Met on this case so it won't take long for them to get a warrant to release all the footage to us. I'm sure that Mr Bah would want you to help and not have us to go to any unnecessary trouble.'

'OK, OK, I'll see what I can do!'

He sat at one of the terminals and his fingers started flying across the keyboard. Molly stood behind him, leaning over to see what he was doing. Less than a minute later he pushed his chair away from the desk and stood up.

'There, you can scroll forward and back using the curser.'

Molly sat in the vacated chair, she moved the timeline to 10.30 AM and started to scroll through the footage. What appeared to be a large truck entered the service area at 10.52, backing up to one of the doors. The driver didn't get out of the vehicle and it was impossible to see anyone in the cab due to the poor nature of the recording.

'Is it Fridays that the rubbish gets collected?' she asked.
'No idea, I'm a computer technician, not a bloody cleaner.'

Kell noted the change of attitude but didn't say anything. If something illegal was going on at the bank, he doubted the young man had anything to do with it and was simply following the instructions he'd been given. It was clear that he was annoyed with himself for not editing the recording for the service area to match that of the main entrance, but probably didn't appreciate how significant it was likely to be.

At 12.06 PM, the truck drove off. The number plate was not visible and it was impossible to tell if anything had been put in the back. Molly stopped the recording and updated Kell on what she'd seen, but this was mainly for the benefit of the technician who would doubtless be reporting back to his bosses as soon as they left.

Kell nodded to Molly to wrap things up.

'Thanks, Adrian, you've been very helpful. Please can you email the recordings from the two cameras between 10.30 and 12.30 and make sure the original recordings aren't deleted. The police may well want to look at them. I'd like them to be in my inbox by the time we get back to our office,' she checked her watch, 'in the next half hour.'

Kell added his thanks and they left without another word being said.

The email with the attachments arrived shortly after they got back to the office on Brick Lane. Molly viewed it again to make sure that it was as she'd requested and if there was anything she'd missed earlier, but it simply showed the truck arriving and then leaving just over an hour later.

'I'm going to update the DS I spoke to at the Met on what we've found. It adds a layer of credence to the fact that this is not just a missing person's case, but the evidence is circumstantial. The only aspect they could pursue is potentially tracking the truck once it left the service area, but with no number plate and not even being able to tell its colour, they might be reluctant to put resources on it.'

'Do you think something bad has happened to Emile?' asked Molly. 'I mean they wouldn't have killed him, would they?'

'Nothing surprises me anymore. But if Emile has been harmed, then he must have known something that they are desperate to keep quiet,' replied Kell. 'Right, I'm going to ring DS Stagg and it might be worth having another word with the girlfriend. She said that Emile wasn't happy with a few things that were going on at the bank, maybe that's the key. Give her a call and see if she can think of anything she's not told us.'

Zornitsa Elianti couldn't add anything to her initial statement and it was just after 6 o'clock when DS Stagg rang Kell back.

When Kell had finished updating him on their progress, the policeman made various non-committal comments. 'Mm, I see. Interesting. That's unusual.'

'I assume you'll want the CCTV footage we've obtained?' Kell was keen to get some involvement from his former employers.

'Yes, I think that's the appropriate next step, although from what you're telling me, it simply confirms that we don't know what time Mr Black left the bank. And the bit about the refuse truck or transit van, well, what are you saying that implies?'

Kell fought hard not to let his frustration show. 'What we know is that Emile Black is missing. No one has heard from him for nearly a week and there is no trace of his phone or bank cards. The CCTV footage is suspicious and suggests the bank is trying to hide something. What this "implies" to me is, that at best Mr Black is being held against his will or worst case scenario has come to some harm.'

'Right, well, thank you, Mr Kell. Send the CCTV footage over and we'll take it from here.'

The call ended and Kell was about to explode in a rage of exasperation when his mobile rang.

'Kell,' he barked as he answered.

'Oh dear, is someone having a bad day,' replied Chris Packham.

'Sorry, yes and it's all your fault. Well, not you personally but the incompetent organisation you work for.'

'Well, why don't we meet for a drink and a bite to eat and you can tell me all about it. Bring Molly as well if she's free.'

'OK, usual place half an hour?' said Kell. 'See you there.'

The Indian restaurant at Monument was as busy as ever but they didn't have to wait for a table. They ordered drinks while Molly perused the menu. The two men decided quickly they'd have the same as usual.

Work matters were avoided in the conversation until they'd finished the main course when between them Kell and Molly recounted the details of Emile Black's disappearance.

When they'd finished, Packham asked, 'Which bank did he work for?'

'Streem, their head office is in Farringdon,' said Molly.

'Oh, well then. That changes everything,' replied the DCI. He thought for a moment. 'This isn't the place to discuss a sensitive case.' He looked at Molly. 'Our new office is nearly ready at Victoria Embankment, but everything is still a mess. I'll come to yours first thing in the morning and we can go through the details.'

*

'The computer guy at the data warehouse, what's his name?' asked Bah, who Canning thought was remarkably calm in the circumstances.

'Adrian Riding, been with us eighteen months. His performance is good. He's a model employee,' she replied.

'And you're sure he didn't tell this Kell guy that you asked him to delete part of the recording?'

'I'm sure, but he is clearly very shaken by the incident. I'd be concerned what he would say to the police if they formally questioned him.'

Canning had a horrible feeling where this was going.

'It seems we have no option. It's imperative that Mr Riding doesn't say anything he shouldn't. It's just a matter of how we achieve it. I'll speak to the others and see what they think. But in the meantime, I suggest you impress on Mr Riding the importance of sticking to his story. We don't want another body on our hands now, do we?'

'Of course, I'll speak to him myself,' replied Canning, who was relieved that she wouldn't be involved with finding a more permanent solution.

With this matter closed for the time being, Bah moved on to the next item on his agenda.

'Is Saul here? We've got to update him on the latest development.'

'Yes, he's waiting in the Board room. You will be interested to know that he got a bit reckless at the casino last Sunday and lost a lot of money.'

Bah smiled as he stood up.

'Excellent.'

11

As Saul sat in the Boardroom at Streem waiting to see his CEO, he knew he should feel elated at how everything in relation to his work life was going. Even though he hadn't officially started his new job, he'd felt he'd settled in quickly, had established good working relationships with his colleagues and he'd been successful in convincing his brother to take over as the Principal of the Wellington School that the bank had bought with a small number of their clients.

As usual, though, the cloud that was hanging over him was his gambling problem. He'd been ridiculously reckless at the casino on Sunday night and for the first time ever he had not only lost all of his available money but had also hit the ceiling of his credit limit at Rupert's. He would have to ask Bah or Canning for the bonus they'd promised him for securing Bill's services and he was already concocting various stories as to why he needed the money.

His thoughts were disturbed by the opening of the door and Bah and Canning walking in looking unnaturally happy.

'Saul, many congratulations. We knew you'd do it. Having Bill on board as the new Principal meant we were able to sign the deal on Monday afternoon,' beamed Bah. 'It was no trouble, Bill is looking forward to the challenge,' he replied.

Bah continued, 'Now, we have to transfer the initial payment this week. This is six million pounds and the bank will receive this money tomorrow from the two primary investors, who are represented by Dirk Paton and Bernice Schmidt who you've met.'

He paused as if he was about to choose his words carefully.

'These investors are key clients for the bank and they choose us for our discretion when handling their financial affairs. In certain circumstances, they prefer if we accept where their money comes from and, how shall I put it, paper over the regulatory checks. We need you to ensure this happens when the funds are processed for the initial payment to the school.'

He looked Saul straight in the eye, clearly expecting a compliant response.

'You do understand what I'm saying, Saul.'

'Er yes, I do. I assume you want me to complete the necessary paperwork,' he replied.

Canning took over. 'Yes, we do Saul. I know this is unusual, but rest assured everything is above board. Your commitment to the bank will be rewarded with the payment of the bonus we promised you. There may be similar circumstances going forward when such discretion is required, but I'm sure you'll agree it's important that we have the confidence of our clients.'

'Yes, I understand. About the bonus—'

Before he could finish, Bah interrupted, 'There is something else I want to discuss. Such is the nature of these deals, that unfortunately two of the minor shareholders, have withdrawn from the transaction. This leaves the syndicate two million pounds short of the balancing payment which is due at the end of the year.'

'But how could you complete the deal, if all the funds haven't been secured?' asked an increasingly nervous Saul.

'That is another matter that we need to overlook and you are now one of only a handful of people who are aware of this. Furthermore, the syndicate would like to offer you and your brother the opportunity to invest. £1m each. You will need to have the funds deposited with the bank by the end of November.'

'I don't have that sort of money and neither does Bill. What makes you think we can come up with £2m in four months?'

'See it as an opportunity. I know you come from a wealthy family, I'm sure you'll figure it out,' replied Bah. 'Oh and the returns will be very attractive indeed.'

'And we don't expect you to try and win it at the roulette table. We're aware of your current financial predicament, so if you want an early payment of your bonus, then I suggest you agree to everything Abebe has said.' Canning's tone had nothing friendly about it at all.

Saul was stunned into silence, sitting there with his head down, not wanting to look them in the eye. He was being asked to be a party to money laundering, no doubt from the proceeds of crime. Such an offence could put him in jail for a long time. If he said no and walked away, what would they do? Then he thought of his predecessor, Emile Black. Had he tried to walk away? He'd always been honest throughout his career, never putting a foot wrong.

This was not just a minor, looking the other way matter. This was a gigantic leap to the dark side and if he took it, then there was no turning back. He had no idea why they would ask him and his brother to invest in the school, maybe it would bind them closer to the illegal dealings, suck him in even further. In any event, they didn't have that sort of money unless their mother relented or they successfully contested the will.

However, on the plus side, there was the prospect of making a lot of money. He had no idea how they knew about his gambling, but they did and without the bonus, he was in deep trouble.

Finally, he looked up. 'OK, I'm in and I won't let you down. But I do need some of the bonus as soon as possible.'

'It will be paid in full and in your bank account tomorrow,' said Canning. 'And I suggest you sort out your gambling problem because the bank will not be your safety net.'

Bah stood up, 'Tomorrow, we are going to the school to meet the management team and relieve the current Principal, Mark Smith from his duties. Your brother will be introduced as the new man in charge and we'll brief him on what we expect. I'll leave it to you to discuss the investment opportunity and I'm sure he'll be excited by the prospect of becoming a shareholder of his place of work.'

Saul stayed in the boardroom, mulling over the crazy events of the last few days. Was this all a set-up from the start? Had they targeted him in view of his family connections? Had they known about his gambling before they offered him the job? In the end, the answers to these questions didn't really matter. He was in and that being the case he was going to make the most of it.

The following day, they travelled separately up to Hertfordshire. Bah went first thing in the morning, driven by his driver, with Saul told he should get there by midday.

When he arrived, he was shown to the Principal's office where Bah and his brother were deep in conversation.

'Ah Saul, I'm just running through the business plan with Bill. You've come at a good time; we're just looking at the feasibility of the growth projections.'

For the next hour, they talked about pupil numbers, changing the fee structure and promoting the school to overseas students.

Saul was relieved when Bah said he had to get back to London. 'You've a lot to think about Bill, but the new board will be there to help you. We'll meet next week to move things on. In the meantime, please make any changes you see fit to the management team. Saul, I need you in the office at 7.30 in the morning before you go to your other job. We're meeting with Francis, re the initial funds and there's an external party I want to introduce you to.'

They shook hands and as soon as Bah left, Bill Solomons let out a long, deep breath as if he'd been holding it for too long. 'He doesn't hang around, does he? Talk about being thrown in at the deep end.'

'He's very dynamic, but that's a trait with most CEOs. He knows what he wants and in this case, it's up to us to deliver,' replied Saul.

'He certainly does. Now, what's the next step as far as you're concerned?' asked Bill.

'There's another side to the purchase that Abebe wanted me to discuss with you personally. An opportunity you could say.'

'Sounds intriguing, I'm all ears.'

Saul had decided that being direct and to the point would be the best approach with his brother.

'There's an opportunity for us to buy a stake in the school. It amounts to approximately 8% each and would cost £2m, that's £1m each to be clear.'

'I haven't got that sort of money, have you?' said an incredulous Bill.

'No, I haven't either, but mother has and we need to convince her quickly. This will change our lives, Bill. We'll never have to worry about money ever again.'

12

There were two versions of the news of the sale of the school, the new ownership, its plans for growing student numbers and ongoing investment. The official press release and the notification to existing students and parents painted a rosy picture of a modernisation programme, improved academic performance and growing pupil numbers particularly from overseas.

The unofficial grapevine within the teaching staff and the summer boarders was more colourful but for different reasons. Mark Smith, the Principal sacked for embezzlement of school funds and having various affairs with both male and female colleagues. Dissatisfied staff, due to ill-disciplined students. Falling pupil numbers, making the school unviable and so on.

For Roddy, Max, Al and Con there was only one topic of conversation as they took a break from repainting the small cricket pavilion. Bill Solomons.

'I can't believe this is happening!' exclaimed Roddy. 'How can he be put in charge?'

'They must be desperate, I doubt he can run a bath without his mum's help, let alone a school,' said Max.

'Every cloud though,' said Con. 'At least, he won't be doing any more teaching.'

'I'm not so sure about that. He can make our final year a complete misery if he chooses to. And I don't think I could stand that,' said Al.

Roddy stood up and walked around his friends. 'We all agree then. We have to get him out of here. It's time to put my plan into place.' He sat back down and gestured to them to come closer until they were sitting cross-legged in a tight circle. By the time Roddy had finished, his three closest friends were thinking the same thing. He had finally lost it. He had undoubtedly gone stark raving bonkers.

*

'I didn't appreciate you had aspirations to become the Head of the school?' said Esther Solomons. 'How long have you known about this? And why haven't you seen fit to tell me about it before now.'

'I don't have to tell you everything about my private life and anyway, I only heard about it myself the other week.'

'Are you capable of running a school?'

'Thanks for your support and encouragement mother and yes, I am capable. If that idiot Smith can get away with it for as long as he did, then I can certainly make a go of it. I'll also have a lot of support from the new owners and—' He was about to tell her of Saul's involvement when she interrupted again.

'And who are these new owners? It seems very mysterious to me when they talk about syndicates and investment. Who in their right minds would want to invest in a school?'

'There's a lot of money to be made in private schools. The fees are going through the roof as the state system crumbles from within. We just need to improve the offering and students will be flocking to us from all over the world.'

'I'll believe that when I see it. Now I must get on. The gardener will be here soon.'

'Mother, there is something very important that I need to discuss with you. Please can you sit down and let me speak without interrupting.'

He didn't often raise his voice, so when he did, he got her attention.

'Very well, I've got ten minutes.'

It took him twenty, to go through the plans for the school, his brother's involvement and the investment opportunity that required £2m. When he finished, she said, 'I've never heard of anything so ridiculous. I can't understand why Saul would get himself involved; he knows less about running a school than you do. And if you think I'll be giving you any money towards such a stupid venture, then think again.'

As she got up and left the kitchen he could hear her muttering, loud enough so he could hear, 'Over my dead body.'

*

Saul was slowly getting used to the very long days. In some ways, he was grateful that by the time he'd finished work at both his jobs he was completely shattered and the itch to go to the casino was dulled by complete exhaustion. It was approaching 9.30 in the evening and he was leaving the office at Streem when his mobile rang. He wasn't surprised to see that it was his brother.

'Bill, how's it going,' he asked.

'You won't be surprised to hear that mother has no intention of letting us have any of father's money. She ridiculed the idea of investing in the school and thinks you in particular should have more sense.'

'I'm not surprised,' replied Saul, as another huge weight landed on his back.

'So, I've spoken to the solicitor Crabtree again and told him we want to proceed with contesting the will. I was at university with him. He's the senior partner of a law firm in St Albans and I've instructed him to assess the likelihood of our successfully contesting the will and releasing what is rightfully ours from the estate.'

'Oh, right, I see.'

Saul was taken aback by his brother's unusual decisiveness.

'I've told him it's urgent and he'll do the initial assessment as a favour. If he thinks we have a case and it goes to court, then that's another matter. We'll need to win just to be able to pay the legal fees.'

'When will he have an idea if we have a case?'

'I've already couriered my copy of the will to his office. He needs to see what it says and get a view from a specialist within his firm. I've arranged to meet him on Saturday in St Albans, so clear your diary as you need to be there.'

Saul was too tired to discuss further. He managed "OK" before ending the call and heading home.

The following morning he was in FD's office at Streem at 7.30 on the dot, where Bah and Francis Hall were waiting.

'Our visitor should be here around 8.30,' said Bah, 'so Francis will take you through the transaction and how the funds will move between various related companies.'

Saul had never spoken at any length to the FD, who came across as aloof, to the point of being unfriendly. He put him in his fifties, with all the usual traits of a finance man, pragmatic and to the point.

With no preamble, Hall went straight into the numbers, sketching out how the initial consideration of £6m was split and its journey through a number of companies and investment vehicles before it reached the bank.

'At this stage, the funds will be sitting with us in twelve lots of £500k. We will not undertake any beneficial ownership checks and you will sign off that the sources are legitimate. At this stage, how we distribute it will depend on the next meeting when our guest arrives.'

'You understand what you need to do, Saul?' asked Bah.

'Yes, if we're not completing any checks then it's just making sure the paper trail stands up.'

For some reason, he felt more comfortable with the idea of breaking the law this morning. Probably because he was expecting his six-figure bonus to be paid later that day.

The desk phone rang. Hall answered with a curt, 'Show him up.'

A couple of minutes later, it was Bah's PA who knocked on the door and showed a tall, dark-haired man in a very smart suit into the office.

Bah greeted him and did the introductions.

'Francis, Saul, this is John Bianchi. He's got a very interesting proposition for us.'

13

Packham arrived just after ten o'clock and went straight to the kettle, filled it with water and turned it on.

Kell greeted his friend. 'Make yourself at home, why don't you.'

'Apologies for being late. I had to get the OK to discuss the Streem business with you. It's just mindless red tape, but it seems we have to get a sign off for everything we do these days. It's all this data protection nonsense. Gets in the way of good, old-fashioned policing.'

He made drinks for the three of them and they settled around the meeting table.

Kell and Molly waited for Packham to begin.

'Right, this is really interesting as far as you're concerned Molly because this is the type of thing you'll be working on when you join us. As Justin will be aware, there's a saying in the force, that if in doubt, follow the money. Follow the money and you'll solve the crime. The problem with the modern-day criminal is that this is getting increasingly harder. The proceeds from crime can be moved around the world with the tap of a keyboard. False businesses, shell companies, offshore investment vehicles, digital currencies, the list goes on and on. However.' He paused as if something important had come into head.

'However, one of the obstacles that the bad guys face, is how they wash their ill-gotten gains back into the legitimate financial system.'

Molly interrupted, 'This is why all the financial institutions have teams of people in their Compliance and Risk departments to make sure they're not being used to clean up the dirty money.'

'Correct,' replied Packham. 'Banks and investment houses can be seriously fined and their directors banned or put in jail if they permit crime proceeds to be laundered through their businesses. The problem we've got is that the criminals are finding more sophisticated ways to beat the system and, in some cases, a far blunter instrument. Which is what we are dealing with here.'

'I think I can see where this is going,' said Kell. 'With the government and the Bank of England wanting more competition in the banking sector, they've encouraged new entrants to come into the market. These have tended to be institutions that have their roots abroad and the concern is they're backed by foreign governments with links to organised crime.'

Molly joined the dots and took over, 'One such bank being our friends at Streem.'

'Precisely,' confirmed Packham. 'We haven't anything concrete on them yet, but there is certainly money, flowing through the bank that doesn't look right. They are on our watch list and with resources so stretched we haven't been able to do a full-blown investigation.'

'So, the fact that our missing person, Emile Black, was the Money Laundering guy at Streem and has disappeared off the face of the earth, means that you now have a formal reason to start your investigation,' said Kell.

'Exactly,' said Packham. 'My problem is that I can't let uniform have all the details. I believe you've been dealing with DS Stagg on Black's disappearance.'

'The man's an idiot. No urgency, no understanding of the implications. I can understand why you don't want to let them loose on this,' said Kell.

'That's partly it, but we also haven't got anyone to spare to take the lead. We're so stretched on all fronts, that despite the seriousness, it's not close to the top of our priorities.'

Packham paused and looked at them both.

'So, part of the reason why I was late is I was getting the sign off and budget for you to lead on this Justin, assisted by Molly. You'll have access to all the intel we have on Streem and some junior resources. As soon as there is any concrete evidence that Black may have been taken against his will, that part of the case will be handed back to CID.'

'We're very happy to take this forward,' said Kell. 'But we need to demonstrate to the people at Streem that the police are leading this. If they think it's just us, we won't get past the receptionist.'

'I've already got that. The three of us will go to see the Abebe Bah, the CEO. A show of strength. I'll lead and make it clear we think Black's disappearance is linked to "other" matters we're investigating. This should get you access to the key people and you can start taking statements immediately.'

'Sounds like a plan,' said Kell, nodding his approval. 'What time are we going over there?'

Packham made a point of looking at his watch. 'No time like the present. I've a patrol car waiting outside, so we can make our presence felt.'

The police car pulled up outside the bank in Farringdon fifteen minutes later, blue lights flashing.

'Pull up onto the pavement and keep the lights on,' Packham said to the driver.

Packham led them into the reception area and flashed his warrant card at the startled receptionist. 'DCI Chris Packham, I'm here to see Abebe Bah.'

'Er, I'm not sure he's in today,' replied the receptionist, who looked at Molly, clearly remembering her previous visit. She was wearing a headset and spoke into the mic after a couple of seconds.

'Is Abebe in today? I've got the police wanting to see him.'

They couldn't hear the reply, but the young lady stood up and took her headset off.

'Just a moment please.'

As per Molly's visit, she walked to a door at the side of the lifts, put her ID card in front of the electronic pad and went through.

She came back a couple of minutes later. 'Mr Bah is just finishing a meeting. He'll be free in five minutes. You can wait in one of the meeting rooms.'

She showed them to the lifts and pressed the button for the second floor.

'I see you've not lost your charm,' said Kell as the lift doors closed.

The banter continued as the lift doors opened and they were greeted by a smiling Abebe Bah, who held out his hand in greeting.

'Mr Packham, welcome to our bank.' He shook his hand and then turned to Kell.

'You must be Justin Kell and Molly Cribbs as well. This is becoming a habit, Miss Cribbs. Please, this way.' He showed into a large room opposite the lift.

'Please, take a seat. Tea and coffee are on the way. Now, how can I help you?' Bah was all smiles and didn't seem at all phased by the intrusion into his day. The refreshments arrived and once they had their drinks, Packham began.

'We've become aware of criminal gangs, trying to access mainstream banks in the city, as a source for laundering the proceeds of crime. This is taking various forms, from opening accounts, both business and private, on one hand, to extortion and bribery on the other. We're reviewing various financial institutions, to make sure they're aware of this activity and to ask you to report directly to our new cybercrime team anything suspicious.' He handed the CEO one of his new business cards.

'Rest assured, Mr Packham, we already have an excellent Compliance and Anti Money Laundering team. Anything suspicious we report through the usual channels.'

'I'm very pleased to hear it.' Packham flicked through his notebook until he found what he was looking for.

'A name has come up in the course of our investigations, now let me see where it is—Emile Black. I believe he headed up your "excellent" Anti Money Laundering team.'

'In what way did his name come up. He wasn't involved in anything underhand, was he?' asked Bah.

'I can't go into details at this stage, but I assume you're aware that Mr Black has disappeared and it's imperative we find him as soon as possible.'

'I know he left our employment recently, but after that, he's of no concern to me.'

'Well, he's very much of concern to us,' replied Packham. 'As this is a multi-dimensional investigation, we've called in the expertise of Mr Kell and Miss Cribbs. They will be taking forward various aspects of the investigations and they should be offered all the assistance you can provide. It's important that there isn't any obstruction to what is a time sensitive investigation.'

Bah, looked at each one of them in turn, his demeanour shifting from his previous bonhomie to one of a wary, trapped animal.

Finally, he said, 'Of course. Anything you need, just ask. Now, you must excuse me, I've an important meeting to get to. I'll ask our HR Director to come in to assist with what you want.'

Once he left, Packham smiled. 'I think he got the message. Now, it's up to you two.'

14

Kell and Molly waited half an hour before Suzie Canning appeared.

'Well, they've had plenty of time to get their ducks in a row,' said Kell, just before the smiling HR Director made her appearance.

'So sorry to have kept you waiting, it's one of those crazy days when everything happens at once. Molly, nice to see you again. And you must be Justin. Pleased to meet you.' She shook their hands, sat down at the table and got straight to the point.

'Now, how can I help you?'

Kell took the lead. 'As you're aware, we are working with the police on the disappearance of Emile Black. His disappearance is now regarded as suspicious and you're the last person to have been with him.'

'I see. I did see him that Friday when he handed his notice in, but I'm surprised that no one else has seen him since.'

'Not as surprised as we are and the Met hold the same view,' said Molly.

Canning ignored the comment.

'How can I help you? I told Molly everything I could when I saw her the other day. I don't think there's anything more that I can add.'

'To begin with, we'd like a list of all Streem's employees who work in this building, together with who was in the office on the Friday when you met with Emile. We'd also like a structure chart of the various departments including the Executive. We would then like to interview all of the people who work with or for Emile. If you could give us a tour of the office, we'll approach them directly when we're ready.' Kell smiled, as he saw the first sign of nerves as the HR Director scribbled down his requests.

'We'll also need an access fob each, so we can move freely around the building,' said Molly.

Quickly regaining her composure, Canning replied, 'That's all pretty straight-forward, give me twenty minutes and I'll be back to show you around the office.' Kell and Molly looked at each other, as Canning stood to leave.

'Time is of the essence,' said Kell. 'It shouldn't take twenty minutes to print off a staff list and a structure chart. Could you show us around now, while you get one of your staff to get us the printouts?'

'OK, follow me.' The reluctance at being told what to do was clear by the body language, as Canning led them out of the meeting room.

The office was basically two large open plan floors where the various departments were seated. Each had its name on a sign that was suspended from the ceiling. The directors had a floor to themselves with what Kell thought were modestly sized offices and the second floor was devoted to meeting rooms of various sizes. The staff lists duly arrived as they concluded the tour.

'If that's everything, I'll leave you to get on,' said Canning.

'Just one more thing. Please, can you show us the basement area. The service area where deliveries are made and the rubbish gets collected from,' asked Kell.

'Why do you want to see that? Hardly any of the staff use it. It's mainly the cleaners and maintenance people.'

'We'd like their details as well please.' Kell was polite but firm. He could sense that Canning was getting increasingly anxious and decided to push her buttons a bit more.

'If you could show us now, please, then we'd like to start the interviews by taking your statement.'

Canning didn't reply but turned and led them the opposite way down the corridor, through a door, then a left turn, through another door which brought them to a large elevator, at what Kell assumed was the back of the building.

Kell went to call the lift by holding his fob against the call button.

'Staff fobs don't work on the service entrance doors or lift. This is restricted to the maintenance people and the cleaners. The Executive also have access, but this seldom happens in practice.'

She called the lift and they went down to the basement area.

'This lift accesses all floors,' she said as she stepped out into a standard underground area.

There was a designated section for the larger industrial-type bins of various colours, indicating the type of waste that should be put in them. Large double doors to the left which said, 'Plant Room,' and a small office near the bottom of a ramp that enabled vehicular access. It didn't have a barrier at the bottom, but Kell could see the shutters at street level as he walked towards the office.

He disturbed a surprised security guard from his crossword and asked him to open the shutters. He walked up to street level and looked up and down the service road. He nodded to himself before returning to Molly and Canning who had waited by the lift.

'Very good. We'll need to see the shift rotas, to confirm who was on duty down here last Friday.'

Canning nodded and they returned to their interview room in silence. As soon as they were seated, Kell began, 'Tell us about the performance issues with Emile, that you told the police and Molly about.'

'Those are confidential, covered by various aspects of employment law. I'm sorry but I can't divulge anything in that area.' Canning smiled, thinking she had scored a point.

Kell leaned forward and rested his arms on the table.

'Within the hour the police will be here with a warrant to search the premises. This gives legal permission for a physical search and also covers all electronic records. So, if you don't want me to inform the police of how you are obstructing justice, then I suggest you start talking.'

He sat back and returned her smile, which was replaced with a look of panic.

'I'm sorry, of course. You get so used to the rules and regulations that I seem to go on autopilot sometimes. Emile was a good employee, very reliable and good at his job. He headed up the Regulatory function and attended the senior management meetings.'

'He wasn't a director then?' asked Molly.

'No. His title was Director of Governance, but he wasn't an actual director. Lots of firms give senior staff "director of" titles, when they're not, proper directors.'

'Are you a proper director?' asked Kell. 'Yes, I am.'

'So, back to Emile. What went wrong if he was such a model employee.'

'It started a few months ago. I'm not sure the best way to describe it really. He started to take a more relaxed approach in a couple of important areas.'

Kell and Molly didn't say anything, waiting for Canning to fill the uncomfortable silence.

'There are certain checks we are required to do when money comes into and goes out of the bank. We use specialist software to flag potential issues, such as large amounts, unusual sources, higher-risk countries and the like. When a transaction is flagged, Emile and his team should undertake further checks to confirm or otherwise that the funds are legitimate. Emile would often do these checks himself. Then the number of cases reported to the National Crime Agency, reduced dramatically, to the point we asked Internal Audit to do a spot check.'

'What did they find?' said Kell.

'The best way to describe it is a lack of thoroughness. Not following up on certain red flags, letting things go that should be looked into further. That type of thing. We had a number of conversations with Emile about it, some unofficial and latterly on the record. It became clear he had issues outside of work. Before you ask, I'm not certain what these are, but he alluded to relationship problems with his partner.'

'Did you conclude that he was intentionally, let's call it bending the rules, for some of the bank's clients?' asked Molly.

'I don't believe so. Following the audit, we reported a number of cases to the NCA but it doesn't appear he was in cahoots with criminals or anything like that. On the Friday I saw him, it seemed like everything had gotten too much for him and he was relieved when I accepted his resignation.'

'Interesting,' mused Kell. 'Did you take him down to reception when he left?'

'No, I called the lift for him, we shook hands and that was the last time I saw him.'

'Do you need your fob to go through the turnstiles at reception?' asked Molly, knowing full well that you did.

'Er yes, you do. If there's a visitor, then reception buzzes them through.'

'So, whoever was on reception would remember letting Emile through the turnstile?'

'I imagine so. I'll find out who was on and you can ask them yourselves.'

'Thanks, that's all very helpful. Is it OK if use the small room opposite as well, to take the statements?' enquired Kell.

'Of course, no problem Now, I really do need to get on.'

When Suzie Canning left, they looked at other with the same concerned expression.

Molly said what they were both thinking. 'So, either Emile Black is involved with the money laundering or it's an elaborate lie, that's trying to turn attention away from the bank itself.'

'Suggesting that Black might be having relationship issues, is a clever move. This adds credence to the fact that he has simply walked away from the relationship and gone somewhere to start afresh. If he is involved with organised crime, then setting him up with a new ID would be relatively straight-forward.'

'I doubt he's important enough for them to do that. And if he's past his sell by date, then they'd either cut him loose or potentially make him disappear, if they thought he could point the finger at them. My hunch is that Ms Canning has spun us an elaborate web of lies but let's see what his colleagues have to say. I'm going to ask around on the floors, you take his team and see what they have to say,' said Kell.

It got to 6 o'clock and Molly had just finished her final interview with Black's team, all of whom had nothing but good things to say about him. It was only his number two, Pedro Sanchez, that had anything interesting to say.

Kell was finishing a call when she walked into the meeting room.

'That was Chris, with some interesting news,' he said. 'How did you get on?'

'OK, only one of his team was able to provide anything useful,' replied Molly.

'Let's debrief over a drink and try and make some sense out of this. There's some nice bars in Smithfield.'

'Whatever you say, boss.'

When they were settled with their drinks, Kell began, 'Most of the staff I spoke to, only knew who Emile was. Would say good morning and the like but didn't know anything about his private life and couldn't comment on his work as they didn't have any dealings with him. The couple that knew him slightly better had no idea he had even left! Can you believe it?'

'It was the same with most of his team, only good things to say. They liked working for him and were disappointed when he resigned.'

'How did they find out he'd resigned,' asked Kell.

'An email went out from HR. I had a look at it. Just the usual bland statement. It was his number two, Pedro Sanchez, whose got specific concerns.'

Molly turned to her notes.

'Sanchez's version is that it was Emile who was getting worried about being pressurised into signing off certain transactions that looked "very dodgy" according to Pedro. He said they were basically bribing him, with a bigger bonus and salary increases to ignore certain concerns that the systems highlighted. Just before he left, he said Emile thought he was going to be fired, which would mean he'd find it very difficult to get another job in the industry. That's why he resigned. Pedro is also looking for another job as he says the culture is toxic.'

'We've a lot to think about and Chris is coming in tomorrow for a full debrief.'

'You said he had some interesting news?' said Molly.

'Yes, they've got a lead on the truck that left the bank in the time window we're interested in. His team are following up and he should have an update by lunchtime tomorrow. Now, let's order some food, I'm starving.'

*

Esther Solomons had always been an early riser, especially in the summer months when it started getting light at 4.30. Her usual routine was up at 6.00 AM, for a stroll around the grounds before a light breakfast at 7.00. She made sure she was on hand to make her eldest son the toast and coffee he usually had, although this last week he'd been staying over in his rooms at the school as he professed to being incredibly busy since his appointment as Principal.

This morning was particularly beautiful, there was already some warmth in the sun and not a breath of wind. As she wandered through the rose garden her thoughts turned to the concern she had with the boys plans to invest in the school, particularly such a large amount.

She would certainly not be letting them access any of their father's legacy for such a ridiculous proposition, although she was weakening in her resolve to stick strictly to her late husband's wishes and not to let them have a penny until her time came to join him in the next life. She could see the tension it was causing between the three of them and now that Saul was visiting a lot more, she didn't want the matter to become a rift between them.

Lost in these thoughts, she turned into the small orchard, stood stock still, froze in shocked terror and screamed. The heads of two foxes hung from a branch of her favourite Egremont Russell. Next to them hung their bodies which had their entails dangling, being feasted upon by crows. The scene was akin to that from a horror movie. She instinctively took a step back and caught her foot on an edging stone, tripped over and everything went black.

15

Saul was first to arrive at the solicitor's office, the traffic out of London being unusually light. He waited outside the office for his brother, who arrived ten minutes later with a man who looked of similar age to themselves, dressed casually in a polo shirt, jeans and smart white trainers.

'Saul, this is Miles Crabtree. Miles, Saul.'

They shook hands and went into the building. They walked up an ornate staircase to the first floor, where Saul was surprised to see a number of people working away at their desks. They followed Crabtree to his office, where a pot of coffee was waiting for them.

When they had their drinks, Crabtree got straight to the point.

'Right, first off, the basics. There are a number of circumstances that provide the basis for a Will to be contested. Some of these are not relevant in your case. For example, where money or property has been promised in return for care and support and has not been carried out within the Will. Or there is a challenge to the legitimacy of the Executor.

The ones that could be applied to your circumstances are that money or property were promised but the details are not contained in the Will or that the Will terms do not fully reflect the wishes of the testator. I mention these because of my initial chat with Bill, as I understand that there were various conversations with your late father about how one day, his estate would be shared between you and that it would assist in whichever direction you wished to take your careers.'

The solicitor paused and looked at each of them to get confirmation that was the case.

Saul nodded his head. 'It wasn't like this was something we discussed all the time. We believed Father to be a healthy seventy-year-old. His death came as a shock to us all. I'm not sure how much mother knew about the content of the Will, but she started talking about it soon after his death, as though she was preparing us, to feel let down.'

Crabtree interjected, 'It is quite usual for a husband and wife to discuss the details of each other's Will, particularly when the estate is being left to the surviving spouse. So, I don't think this aspect is particularly useful in this instance. On how many occasions did your father indicate that you would be included in his Last Will and Testament?'

It was Bill who answered, 'It's hard to put a specific number on it but it did come up in conversation from time to time over a number of years. I think I speak for Saul as well when I say that we both believed we would be left with something substantial. Obviously, Mother would get the house and more than enough to keep her comfortable, but we honestly thought we'd get something.'

'OK, that gives us something to work on. And just remind me when it was he passed?'

'December last year, so eight months ago,' replied Bill.

'OK, well the timing is fine and we do have a potential case, but I'd counsel that you consider very carefully as to whether you proceed. There are the legal fees of course and the natural upset it will cause within the family. Also, your mother's legal team could make sure the case is dragged out well beyond your deadline.'

The brothers looked glum. The message they were hearing loud and clear was that it could all be an expensive waste of time.

Saul broke the silence, 'How much would it cost to prepare our claim and make a statement of intent that we are prepared to pursue the case through the courts? This might make Mother understand that we feel we have a genuine grievance and she'll choose to let us have the funds for the investment.'

'Our fees would be modest,' replied Crabtree. 'I can get a junior solicitor to prepare the papers, so no more than £1000.'

'What do you think, Bill? We can go and see mother now and let her know we are reluctantly taking this course of action and see if she relents. If not, she might think again when she receives the papers.'

'Very well, please proceed, Miles. I'll email you the details of the family solicitor. I assume you can contact them next week?'

'Yes, I'll make sure they get sent out on Tuesday. Now if that's everything, I'm meeting my wife for a bit of shopping and then some lunch. You're welcome to use my office if you want to stay to chat things through. There'll be someone here most of the day. And help yourselves to coffee.'

With the solicitor gone, Bill asked his brother, 'You sure you want to go through this. It'll cause an awful lot of upset?'

Saul had thought long and hard about whether to share the darker side of the purchase of the school with his brother, especially in the light of meeting with the mysterious John Bianchi. These were very dangerous people he'd got himself involved with and he couldn't see any option other than to go along with everything they wanted him to do.

But was now the time? Was there another way to get their hands on £2m in a matter of months? He thought about the tax-free bonus he'd just received and the burning itch to be sitting at the roulette table. Maybe there was, but it would be very much a last resort.

'We won't take it all the way, but we need to take this first step. The money doesn't mean anything to her, it's just the stupid principle of honouring Father's wishes that she's bothered about,' he paused and decided to bite the bullet.

'Look, there's something else you need to know about all this.'

'What's that then?' asked Bill.

'Doesn't matter, another time. Let's get this over with.'

On the drive over to the family home, Saul replayed the meeting with Bah, Francis Hall and the American, John Bianchi in his head. The whole situation was like something out of a crime series on the TV and he was struggling to believe it was happening to him.

The first thing that was clear, was the price being paid for Wellington was overstated and this was somehow being hidden in the transaction. From the initial £6m that would be paid in the next few days, only £4m was being paid to the vendors. The "additional" £2m, were funds the bank had received and noted as being part of the purchase price, but would now be directed into a cryptocurrency, controlled by Bianchi's organisation.

This £2m would remain invested with Bianchi and eventually returned to the bank as "clean" money in the next few months. It was clear this was why the £2m from him and Bill, would be needed as part of the final payment at the end of the year.

The new owners, which included the bank and, of course, him and his brother, would be falsely inflating the student numbers and passing up to £1m per month to Bianchi, to launder through his digital currency. Francis Hall, the FD, had it all worked out. The school was simply the respectable face of a complex money laundering operation that would wash millions of pounds through the financial system.

He wondered how he'd got himself involved in something so illegal and his thoughts kept returning to his predecessor and the actual reasons why he left so suddenly. Could he keep all of this from his brother? As they pulled into the drive of the family home, he decided that for the time being, the answer was yes.

The first indication that something was not quite right was when they saw Mrs Buckle's old Ford Fiesta parked in front of the house. She didn't usually work at the weekend, so they both felt concerned as she hurried out to greet them.

'Thank goodness you're here. She's had a terrible shock and is very distressed.'

'What happened?' asked Bill.

'In the garden, by the orchard. See for yourselves. It's horrible. Why would someone do such a thing.'

They hurried round the side the of the house and ran into the small orchard. The foxes' heads and bodies had continued to be gorged on by the birds and it was hard to distinguish what type of animal they actually were. Once they understood what they were seeing. They ran back into the house, to find their mother in the kitchen adding coffee beans to the peculator.

'What brings you two here at the weekend? Did Mrs Buckle call you? I'm not an invalid you know. I can look after myself.'

'What happened?' was all Bill could manage.

Esther sat at the kitchen table and ran through the morning's events.

'I think I fainted but didn't bang my head, so there's no need to bother the doctor. I assume it was some sad person playing a sick joke. At first, I was shocked and felt sorry for the poor animals, so I rang Mrs Buckle. She advised I should leave the poor things there and call the police. But I don't want any fuss. Albert's coming over to cut them down and dispose of them.'

'Now what are you doing here?'

Seeing that she was alright and being her typical self, despite the alarming situation, Saul bit the bullet.

'Bill and I have been to see a solicitor.'

16

They were both surprised that their mother remained silent whilst between them they reiterated their stance on their late father's will and how if she didn't change her view on letting them have a proportion of their share, then they would commence legal action to contest it.

Finally, she broke her silence. 'I'm going to choose my words very carefully, to make sure I don't say anything I'll regret later. This subject has caused me a lot of stress since your father died. I've been resolute in ensuring I respected his wishes as he left me that responsibility. I will not break that trust now or at any time in the future. That you have chosen to inform me of your intentions today, considering the shock I've had, I find unfathomable. Now, please leave. I'm going to my room to rest.'

She didn't look at either of them as she got up and walked out of the kitchen.

Saul stood where he was shaking his head. Bill sat at the table and put his head in his hands.

'Christ, Bill, what have we done?' said Saul. 'She's never going to speak to us again after this.'

Whether it was the years of the constant nagging and put-downs he'd had or simply the fury that had built up in him over the years, Bill had had enough.

'To hell with her! I'll speak to Miles first thing Monday. If she wants a war, she's got one.'

They were so focused on the money and their mother's reaction that they completely forget about the sick killing of the two foxes.

*

Alexander Stewart, Maksim Orlov and Connor O'Clery were getting concerned about the increasingly erratic comportment of their friend. This latest request for them to meet at the ungodly hour of seven thirty was an example of how strange Roddy's behaviour was becoming.

'If he's not here in the next five minutes, I'm going back to bed,' said Max.

'Me too, this is getting ridiculous, the way he's carrying on,' replied Al.

Always the voice of reason, Con said, 'Look, let's hear what he's got to say, then take things from there. I agree all the religious stuff he keeps quoting is getting more and more bizarre, but he's our friend and if he needs help, then it's down to us.'

At that moment, the door of their Common Room, burst open and there was Roddy looking like he'd been dragged through a hedge backwards and breathing heavily like he'd just sprinted the hundred metres. In the last few months, he'd let his hair grow down to his shoulders and it was matted to his head with sweat from whatever he'd been up to.

'Good, you're all here,' he managed to say through deep gulps of air. 'I've completed stage one of the crusade and it was a great success!'

'What crusade?' asked an irritated Max.

'The crusade against the pagan that is Solomons,' replied Roddy who was slowly getting his breath back.

'Look, mate. I think all this religious stuff is madness. Why is Solomons a "pagan" and more importantly what have you done?' asked his closest friend Al.

Roddy ignored the religious reference, spread his arms like Christ the Redeemer and recounted how he had caught, gutted and beheaded two foxes and then strung them up in the Solomons orchard.

'My plan is to bestow ten plagues on the family like the Lord did with the Egyptians, only then will we be free from the slavery inflicted by Solomons.'

Max couldn't contain himself and started laughing. It was infectious, quickly spreading to the other two. Eventually Al managed, 'I don't remember reading about beheaded foxes in Exodus and I don't think there are any new-born babies in the doc's family.'

Ignoring the laughter and cynicism Roddy continued, 'This was just a taster; I will deliver the second plague next week. And if you had studied the scriptures properly Al, you would know that the final plague was the death of the first borns' and that means William Solomons.'

Max had heard enough. 'I'm sorry, man, I'm out. You've lost it mate. I don't want anything else to do with you and your mad plans. I'm going back to bed.'

As they watched him leave the Common Room, Al put his arm around his friend.

'Come on, mate, let's sit down and talk about this nonsense. You can't go around killing innocent animals and talking about murdering the new Principal of the school.'

Roddy had a dazed look as he sat next to his best friend with Con looking on.

'I know it must be difficult for you to understand but God has spoken to me. I've had visions of what he wants me to do. Solomons is an evil man and we must rid the world of evil. I have been given this task and shown the way to complete it.'

He sounded completely lucid and serious but maybe that's how all how mad people convinced you they are sane, thought Al.

In an attempt to find a connection, Con said, 'But any killing is breaking the law and doesn't the bible say thou shalt not kill?'

'When the Lord was angry with the Egyptians, he inflicted ten disasters on them in which many died. The Bible is full of contradictions but when the Lord speaks you must act or be forever doomed to the fires of Hell.'

Con too had heard enough. 'Right, that's enough for me, you're crazy man. Now we've finished our punishment, I'm heading back home to Ireland for the rest of the summer and Max is coming with me. Al, it's up to you? You coming or not?'

Al looked at Roddy who seemed oblivious to the conversation. 'I can't leave him like this, he needs help. I'm going stick around and see if I can make him see sense, maybe talk to a shrink or something.'

'OK, good luck. See you both at the start of next term.'

When Con had left, Al put his arm around his friend. 'Come on mate, let's have a shower and some breakfast and then we are going to have a serious conversation.'

Al thought he saw a moment of lucidity in Roddy's eyes when he nodded his head. 'Sure, I desperately need to change these clothes.' It was short-lived as he continued, 'Where will we find a load of frogs? I think we'll need at least five hundred.'

Once his friend had showered and put on clean clothes, he looked a lot better and Al noticed a calmness in his demeanour. They sat in the canteen eating cereal and toast and drinking lukewarm sweet tea. The conversation touched on Con and Max going back to Ireland to stay with Con's family, but not the reasons why they'd chosen to go. Finally, Al decided to take the direct approach.

'Look, Roddy, I'm concerned about you. You're acting very strangely and I'm worried for your mental health with this fixation on Solomons. Do you want to talk about it?'

Roddy put down his mug of tea and brushed his long hair away from his face.

'I've been doing a lot of reading, studying different religions, different perspectives and to be honest, I'm finding it confusing and very worrying. I think the best way to describe it, is like when you think what it would be like if the world never existed. If there was no planet, no earth, no life and there was just nothing. I often think back through history and even in the hundreds of years that I've studied, millions if not billions of people have died.

So, you tell me, do you think they all in heaven or hell or wherever, surely there can't be enough room? And then, to explain all this man invented all these different religions. But they can't all be right so who do you believe?'

He paused and took a sip of his now cold tea.

'I've been trying to work out which one is real and it's very difficult. In our bible, my favourite books are Exodus in the Old Testament, which is where I got using the ten plagues theme for scaring Solomons away. And in the New Testament its Revelation, the four horsemen and all that. But I'm finding it really hard to decide what I should believe in.'

'Do you have to believe in any of it?' said his friend. 'Lots of people ignore religion, I think they're called atheists or agnostics or something. Can't you just enjoy being alive and having fun?'

'I know you think I'm mad but I'm not. I feel like I'm searching for the truth and sometimes it's like it's so close I can almost touch it,' he sighed and looked at his best friend.

'Look, I'll dial it back on the Doc. No more pranks. It's only one more year and we're out of here. But I am going to continue my quest for the truth. I plan to study theology and religion at Uni, probably abroad. Talking of which, a book I requested has come into the library.'

And without another word he left, leaving Al even more convinced that Roderick Roan was definitely losing it, but with no idea what he could do about it.

17

They were in the office early the next day, typing up their notes from the interviews at the bank.

'The thing is,' said Kell. 'That until we find Emile, hopefully alive, all we've got is a mountain of circumstantial evidence.'

'Chris and his team should be able to get something tangible on the money laundering at the bank,' said Molly.

'But if they do then they've set Emile up as the perfect fall guy. It's pretty clever really.'

'It's not just about one person though. We covered this in my degree. All the directors have responsibility to ensure that the systems and controls operated within a financial institution are robust enough to stop any financial crime from being committed. They generally focus on the most senior people, so I think our next step should be interviewing Bah and his FD.'

Kell nodded, 'Agreed. But let's see what Chis says. He might want his guys to do that when we've updated him. He should be here any minute, so let's see what he's got on the lorry and we'll take it from there.'

It was 11.30 by the time Packham arrived.

'Why do you always come here Chris? Wouldn't it be easier if we came over to the station?' asked Molly.

'There's simply far too much bureaucracy getting anyone in at the moment. There are countless online forms you have to submit that go up the chain of command and they get stuck if someone happens to be out. It's a bloody nightmare. Anyway, the coffee is much better here.'

'I'll take that as the cue to put the kettle on,' said Kell.

'How's the flat hunting going? Have you found anything yet?' asked Packham.

'Been too busy. Anyway, there's no rush, we're quite settled at mine at the moment,' replied Kell.

Kell brought their drinks over and Packham pulled out his police-issued tablet and got back to the matter in hand.

'This is the CCTV footage of the van that visited the bank in the timeframe we're interested in.' They stood behind him bending over so they could see the grainy footage.

'The tech guys have got a cleaner version, but what we're seeing is an unmarked white transit van, with no company logos. The number plate confirms it's one of a job lot that's leased by a haulage company in Essex. They're used by various businesses in the Greater London area, delivering anything from computer equipment, office furniture even stationery. My guys are over there as we speak establishing the reason for the visiting the bank that morning. They'll ring me as soon as they have anything.'

'How far were you able to follow it?' asked Molly.

'It headed out on the A127. The coverage stops when you get to the countryside between Billericay and Basildon. And before you say anything, Justin, we've got the local force checking for any businesses and the like it could have been making for. But we really need to talk to the driver. Now, how did you get on yesterday.'

Kell let Molly run through the details and answer his friend's questions. When she'd finished, they waited for Packham to finish scribbling his notes.

'Right, my brief from the top brass, is to pursue all this as two separate cases. Clearly, the disappearance of Emile Black is a priority and resources are being prioritised accordingly. However, there's a bigger play going on with the bank itself and its links to organised crime. Money laundering is one of the focuses, but the waters got a bit murkier yesterday when I was informed that a certain John Bianchi arrived at Heathrow on the redeye from New York.'

'I recognise that name,' said Molly. 'Didn't he have something to do with that case of the missing Canadian and all the stuff that went on in Manchester?'

'Correct. He was certainly in the country at the time, although we can't say for sure he was involved in any way. He hides behind a veneer of respectability these days, with various legitimate businesses in New York and on the West Coast.

We also believe he controls the digital currency, Mandara, which whilst not illegal in itself, is increasingly being used by organised crime across the world as a means of cleaning the proceeds of their illegal activities. We have also established that Bianchi is in contact with Abebe Bah at Streem, so the case has the potential to catch some very big fish.'

'What's your next move?' asked Kell.

'We are working with the regulators, primarily the FCA. They've analysed Streem's regulatory reports since they became authorised and have concluded, that their financial position has been significantly misrepresented. They are ready to undertake a supervisory visit to the bank and we propose to let this proceed. This will commence on Monday. We also have intelligence that the bank is part of a consortium that has just purchased a private school in Hertfordshire, The Wellington.'

'Why would a bank want to buy a school?' asked Molly.

'Good question,' replied Packham. 'This particular school is what you'd call a middle-of-the-road establishment. It's not up there in the premier league, but it does have a decent reputation. The prospectus published by the owners, lays out big plans for investment in the school, new buildings, infrastructure, the best academics to teach there and so on.'

Kell interrupted, 'And the better the school and the offering, the more fees you can charge. The key is for them to attract overseas students. Once you've done that, you can basically charge what you like.'

Packham laughed. 'Very good, Justin, you'd have made a good detective, if you'd stayed with us.'

Ignoring the jibe, Kell said, 'So, the conundrum is, do you wait on the FCA investigation or do you go charging into the school and start pulling apart the deal?'

'Exactly, which is why we need to crack on with finding Emile Black. He is crucial in throwing some light on what's happening at Streem,' said Packham.

'If he's alive, that is,' replied Kell.

They were quiet whilst they digested the very real possibility that this might be the case.

Kell broke the silence. 'Right, if it's OK with you, Chris, we've got more interviews we need to do at the bank. There's the cleaning and maintenance staff, particularly the guy who was manning the security hut in the service area on the day Emile disappeared. We also want to speak to the CEO, Bah and his FD. What's his name, Mol?'

'Francis Hall,' she replied. 'Actually, there is someone else I think we should talk to.'

'Who's that?' they both asked.

'His name is Saul Solomons. He's Emile Black's replacement. They somehow managed to recruit him very quickly. He's due to start on 1 September, but I noticed he was on the structure chart as helping with Project Waterloo, whatever that is?'

'Now, that's very interesting,' said Kell.

They looked at him in anticipation.

'I assume that neither of you studied history beyond GCSE.'

They both shook their heads.

'The Battle of Waterloo, June 1815. The final defeat of Napoleon Bonaparte. Arthur Wellesley commanded the British army, which included Dutch and German troops. And you know who Arthur Wellesley was?'

Another shake of their heads.

Kell smiled, 'He was the Duke of Wellington. Hence the project name for the school acquisition. So, let's make talking to Mr Solomons a priority. Mol, please find out as much as you can about the Wellington and then let's go and find Mr Solomons.'

18

Packham checked his watch. 'I've got time to come to the bank with you. I can't stay long, but it'll show them that we're taking Emile's disappearance seriously.'

They collected the files they needed and headed down to the car that was waiting for the Detective Chief Inspector.

They got a friendly greeting from the lady on reception, who signed them in and gave Packham an entry fob.

'Please, could you ask Ms Canning to join us in the meeting room,' said Kell.

They'd just got their tablets and notepads out when a smiling Suzie Canning breezed in. There was the briefest look of concern as she welcomed the DCI, but she quickly settled back into what Kell thought was an out-of-character charm offensive.

'Did you have a successful day yesterday?' she asked.

'Yes, we did thank you,' replied Kell. 'We've briefed the Detective Chief Inspector and he would like to lead the interviews with Mr Bah and Mr Hall, I assume they're in the office today?'

'Er, yes they are, but I'm not sure what meetings they've got.'

Packham interrupted, 'I'm sure they can spare half an hour in view of the urgency of the situation. Obstructing a police investigation is a serious matter.'

'I'll see if they're free.'

As she stood up, Kell asked, 'Saul Solomons, is he in today?'

'No, he doesn't join us until the 1 September.'

'But his name is on the structure chart you gave us as working on Project Waterloo,' said Kell.

'Saul is working his notice with his current employer. We keep him updated on various ongoing matters that we're working on so he can hit the ground running when he starts. It's not like he's here in the office at all, although occasionally he does pop in, in the evenings.'

'As you are in contact with him, could you ask him to come and see us here this evening. If that's not convenient, then he can come down to the station tomorrow,' Packham's tone was firm.

'I'll see if I can get hold of him. Now if you'll excuse me, I'll see if Abebe and Francis are available.'

'I didn't know you worked evenings,' quipped Kell.

'I don't but you do! I doubt he's in any way involved with Black's disappearance, so you'll have to tread carefully. I don't want him to think we've any real interest in the school at this stage, but the speed of his appointment is unusual. So, just sound him out on how he got the job and any connection with his predecessor.'

'Yes, boss,' said Kell. 'Molly, do you want to take the cleaning staff and talk to whoever was on duty in the service area when Emile disappeared. And do a background on our friend Saul Solomons.'

'OK, but I expect the cleaners won't start work until late afternoon.'

'Good, I'd like to speak to CEO so if you could take the FD, Justin, what's his name again?' asked Packham.

'Francis Hall,' said Molly.

'Right, I'll have to head straight back to the station after I've spoken to Bah, so could you both come over first thing in the morning. I'll arrange a debrief with the full team.' With perfect timing, Suzie Canning reappeared. 'Francis and Abebe can see you now.'

'Thank you, I'd like to speak to Mr Bah and Justin will see Mr Hall.'

Bah's office door was open and he was seated at his desk when Packham walked in. 'Thank you for seeing me at short notice, Mr Bah.'

'You're welcome, Chief Inspector, anything I can do to be of help. Do you have any news on where Emile might be?'

'We are pursuing a number of leads and anticipate a breakthrough in the next couple of days.'

'Sounds very promising, now how can I help you?'

'Ms Canning has made a statement that there were concerns with Emile's performance, specifically in the area of completing the required anti-money laundering checks. How did the Board respond to these concerns?'

'It appeared that Emile had some problems in his personal life and that was affecting his work. We always try and support our staff through such times, but Emile's performance did not improve and his lack of focus exposed the bank to a significant risk of an intervention by the Regulator.'

'What were these personal issues?' asked Packham.

'I'm not fully aware of the details, but I understand there were problems at home.'

'Do you think he could have been pressurised by a third party to fudge some of the checks?'

'What sort of third party?'

'Individuals who didn't want the source of their funds becoming known—' He didn't finish his sentence as his mobile rang.

'Apologies, but this could be important.'

'Packham. Yes. When. Where. OK, I'm on my way.'

He put the phone back in his pocket and looked Bah in the eye. 'The Essex Police have found a body. They believe it could be Emile Black.'

He got up and left the stunned CEO in his office and went to the next room, where Kell was interviewing Francis Hall.

'Justin, we've found a body. I've got to go. Finish up here and we'll meet in the morning as discussed.'

'What was all that about?' asked the Finance Director.

Kell replied, 'If it's Emile's body they've found, then it's no longer a missing person investigation, it's a murder enquiry. We'll have to finish this another time.'

He didn't feel the need to spell out the obvious, as he got up and went to find Molly.

*

At the casino, Saul arranged extended credit up to £50k when he played on a private table. He had to show to proof of funds and consent to a credit check but as he'd paid off his credit card and didn't have any other loans that were of concern to the General Manager, it was quickly approved.

By playing on a private table, the casino could track his position on each spin of the wheel. From Saul's perspective, this was a perfect arrangement. Whilst he fully expected to win, in the unlikely event that he did happen to lose, he simply settled up at the end of the evening.

It was late afternoon and he was sitting in his office going through his recent reports to the Audit Committee, with his interim replacement. The handover was going well and he was hoping they'd put him on gardening leave, for the last three weeks of his notice. His mobile rang, showing it was his brother.

He didn't bother excusing himself, he was still the boss after all. 'Hi, Bill, what's up?'

'They application to contest the Will has been filed. Miles is pushing for the initial hearing as soon as possible. Have you heard anything from Mother?'

'That's good, but no, haven't heard a thing.'

'It's just that I'm so busy at the school, I'm staying here and haven't been home in a few days. On top of that, my car wouldn't start the other day, so it's stuck on the drive at home.'

'Look, we've got the Exec Meeting on Friday. I'll be driving up, so I'll take you back to the house and we can have another chat with her. Hopefully, she'll see we're serious and we can avoid the unpleasantness of a hearing.'

'OK, I'll see you then. Bye, Saul.'

The call ended and he checked the time on his phone. 'Right, I think that's enough for today. Unless you've any questions, I'll see you in the morning.'

It was 5 o'clock and he'd had an urgent message from Suzie Canning to call in at Streem.

The receptionist greeted him with warm smile. 'You're to go straight to the boardroom.'

'Thanks, who's up there?'

'Mr Paton and Miss Schmidt arrived earlier, so it must be something important.'

He got in the lift hoping it wouldn't take too long and disrupt his plans at the casino.

There was an animated conversation taking place as he walked in. As well as Dirk Paton and Bernice Schmidt, there was Bah, Hall and Canning sitting at the far end of the large oval table.

'Good, you're here,' said Bah. 'There's been various developments that we need to update you on.'

Saul sat down and waited for the CEO to continue.

'You are probably not aware, that following his resignation from the bank, your predecessor, Emile Black went missing. His girlfriend informed the police and they assumed he had decided to split up from his partner as there were some issues in the relationship. Earlier this afternoon I met with a Detective Chief Inspector Packham who informed that the police had found a body in Essex. It has still to be formally identified, but they believe it to be Emile Black.' He paused to let the news sink in. 'As you can imagine, we are all in shock.'

'Did he kill himself?' asked a stunned Saul.

'It is too early to say. But—'The CEO looked around the room as if to make sure he had everyone's attention.

'The police implied that they had information that suggested Emile was working for a third party who were pressurising him to turn a blind eye on certain of the regulatory checks.'

Saul went white as the events of the last few weeks fell into place. The speed of his appointment, his brother being at the school, where the funds originated from for the purchase, his being asked to doctor some of the checks, the ridiculously large bonus he'd been given and being on the line for sourcing the £2m shortfall. He felt physically sick.

The American, Dirk Paton, got up, walked around the table and sat directly opposite Saul.

'I see you understand the seriousness of the situation Saul. Bernice and I represent some very, let's call them influential people. We won't let our businesses' interests be interfered with by anyone. So, we need to be convinced that you're 100% on board. Do I make myself clear?'

They waited for him to answer.

Of all the crazy stuff that was going on, only one thing came into his head.

'Was it you who had Emile Black killed? Are you the third party who was pressuring him?'

Saul was surprised when it was Hall, the FD who answered.

'Mr Black was happy to go along with a liberal interpretation, of applying some of the regulatory requirements. Like yourself, he was being appropriately rewarded. Unfortunately, he got greedy and gave us an ultimatum we could not accept.'

He looked around the room.

'We are the only people who have the full picture. Moving money around the financial system happens all the time. It is a victimless crime, unless of course, someone overplays their hand. And I understand you are well aware of how that can turn out.'

Canning took over. 'The demise of Emile Black is not your concern. You didn't know him, didn't work with him, knew nothing about his personal life. All you have to do is continue to falsify certain AML checks and you will earn more money than you ever imagined. Probably enough to fund your gambling habit.'

Again, Saul was lost for words. They were still waiting for his answer and all he could manage was.

'And the £2m? Do we still have to get that?'

Bah: 'Yes, that's part of the deal.'

Canning: 'We want you to think very carefully, what you say next Saul. We need your 100% commitment to the Bank. This is a life-changing moment for you.'

Despite his bewilderment, he understood the inference of what she said. He looked up and glanced around the room.

'Of course, I'm in. You can rely on me, I promise.'

'That's good news, Saul, because the police are downstairs and want to talk to you.'

19

Roddy sat on his bed in their dormitory, a shaft of sunlight lighting up his face. There was no one else around, which was just the way he liked it. He was thinking. Not meditating as some people like to call it. Just simple thinking and he had a lot to think about. He was also very tired. He'd done so much reading in the last few weeks, often into the early hours of the morning, then waking up at six or seven with only a few hours of disturbed dreams to replenish his body.

It was the dreams he spent his first few wakeful hours thinking about. He couldn't always remember all the details, but once he'd got the gist of what they were about, he let his imagination fill in the blanks. He'd concluded that dreams were how God spoke to people. After all, how else could it be? God didn't suddenly start whispering in your ear or send you a note about what he wanted you to do. No, he didn't. It was in the dreams that He gave you your instructions.

It wasn't a dream that told him old Doc Solomons was a bad person. He'd decided that himself in his first year at Wellington and the realisation had grown week on week, month on month, year on year. He remembered most of the things that Solomons had called him. Initially, it had been "daydreamer, head in clouds, naïve little boy", at the politer end of the scale. Then a "waste of space, useless and a nasty little shit" were just a few of the more recent descriptions bestowed on him by the newly appointed Principal of the school.

Solomons didn't like his friends either. But the vitriol of his dislike of their group was focused on him. He was their de facto leader and was always singled out by Solomons for the most severe punishment. He'd even been caned across his backside by the tyrant.

But that was all behind him because now it was his turn. It wasn't a surprise that his friends had deserted him. They'd never had the stomach for the fight. OK, Al had not run away when things were heating up, but he knew their friendship was not the same and that what he planned to do next, he'd have to do on his own. But what?

His idea of mirroring the plagues of Egypt was proving difficult. It was impossible to get hold of loads of locusts or frogs and he couldn't control the weather or create darkness. He'd concluded that in guiding him to the plight of the Israelites in trying to leave Egypt, God had provided "examples" of the type of punishments that would be appropriate for Solomons and that it was up to him to decide his fate. His dream from last night had provided how the final retribution would be delivered, it was just a matter of finalising the details.

*

Bill Solomons was enjoying the challenge of his responsibilities of overseeing the school. For the last week, he'd been pouring over the business plan provided by the bank and whilst student numbers wouldn't increase significantly for the forthcoming academic year, the last-minute increase in fees had resulted in a numerous queries from parents and guardians. He'd dealt with most of these personally.

On the one hand, he wanted to introduce himself as the new Principal but also because the rest of the senior team hadn't yet seen all the details of the ambitious expansion plans. The bank had appointed a new bursar, who was due to start later that day. The banking arrangements had already been switched from HSBC to Streem and he'd been assured that this was an area he didn't need to get involved with in detail.

He'd just finished a call with a parent explaining the improvements the school had planned when there was a knock on his office door.

'Come in.'

His secretary put her head around the door. 'There's a student who wants to see you, Bill.'

'Not now, Helen, I'm up to my ears in figures and phone calls. Ask them to make an appointment for later in the week.'

'He says it urgent.' She paused, 'It's Alexander Stewart.'

In all the years that Stewart and his awful friends had been at the school, not once had any of them asked to see him or any of his colleagues. His interest piqued, he said, 'OK, send him in.'

With Con and Max having gone home, Al had no one to discuss the problems that were manifesting in Roddy. He knew his friend was ill and more than likely on the verge of doing something stupid that would almost certainly hurt someone including himself, but who could he turn to?

Eventually, he concluded that much as he didn't like the guy, Solomons was his only option, he was after all the target of Roddy's ongoing vendetta. But how much should he divulge? He was turning all this over in his mind when he found himself outside the Administration Office. The door was open, but he knocked anyway and waited to be asked to enter.

'How can I help you, Alexander?' asked Mrs Turner. 'I'd like to see Mr Solomons if he's available?'

'And what is it concerning.'

'Er, it's a personal matter, actually. I'd rather not say,' replied Al. 'Very well, I'll see if he's free.'

Moments later, he was standing in the Principal's office. He heard Mrs Turner closing the door behind him and for a split second, he felt trapped like a caged animal.

'Please take a seat, Alexander.' Solomons gestured to one of the two chairs in front of his large oak desk.

'Please can you call me Al. I hate being called Alexander.'

'Of course. Just like the Paul Simon song. Now, how can I help you, Al?'

They sat staring at each other momentarily before Al responded.

'It's about Roddy. I don't think he's very well.'

'And what is the matter with Roddy. Has he seen the nurse?'

'I don't think it's anything the nurse can help him with. It's just that he's been acting really strange recently.'

'I don't think that's so unusual for Roan,' said Solomons. As soon as the words were out of his mouth, he knew he'd made a big mistake.

Al stood up to leave. 'Bloody typical. We know you don't like us, especially Roddy. I should have known you wouldn't be any help.'

'OK, I'm sorry. I shouldn't have said that. It was wrong and insensitive. And for the record it's not you and your friends I disapprove of, it's your behaviour. There's a huge difference in the two.'

Al sat back down. And looked quizzically at the Principal, processing what he'd just said.

'Aren't they the same thing?'

'Absolutely not. I'm sure that each of you are perfectly fine young men and will go on to achieve great things. Behaviour is what you do, how you act. For example, setting fire to a curtain in the Assembly Hall. That's bad behaviour is it not?'

'Mmm, I see where you're coming from, I think. So, you don't hate us then?'

'Far from it. All the staff here at Wellington want you to succeed. You've made it difficult for us on occasion, but we all hope that when you leave at the end of the forthcoming year, you'll all be on the paths you've chosen. Whether, that's University, going straight into work or maybe a gap year.'

'You think gap years are a good thing? I'd have thought you'd consider them a waste of time,' said Al.

'Not at all. Taking a break from the academic world and having the time to think about what you want to do with your life is a wonderful thing. Going to different places and experiencing different cultures will only expand your mind and your horizons. Put it this way, I wish gap years had been fashionable when I was your age. I probably wouldn't have ended up teaching.'

'Don't you like being a teacher? I thought it was a vocation, what with being in charge and telling people what to do!'

Solomons laughed. 'It's not like that all. My problem was that I drifted into teaching. It wasn't a positive choice that I made, it just seemed to happen. I really loved my subjects, English Literature, RE and History. In fact, I still love them. The challenge for me is that I don't particularly like teaching them.'

'Now you're the Head, you won't have to do any teaching, so that's good isn't it?' asked Al.

'Yes, that's true and I'm enjoying the challenge even though it's only early days. Now, we seem to have gotten off the subject. You wanted to talk about Roderick.'

'Actually, you've been a great help. I think I know how to help him myself, maybe get him to see the nurse in the first instance.'

He stood up to leave. 'Thank you, Sir. I enjoyed our chat. Er, could I come back another time and we can just talk?'

'Of course, just make an appointment with Mrs Turner.'

Solomons smiled as he watched Alexander Stewart leave his office. Perhaps teaching wasn't such a bad profession after all.

20

It was a sunny, warm August day, so Al decided to walk across the sports fields and reflect on his meeting with Solomons. He was surprised by how easily he'd been able to chat with him and some of the things he'd said had stuck a chord. *It's not you and your friends I disapprove of, it's your behaviour. There's a huge difference in the two.*

He didn't quite understand the difference between a person and their behaviour, surely, they were the same thing. But what he did know was that Solomons came across as a genuine guy, even encouraging the idea of a gap year, which was something he personally was thinking about. Maybe he would go back and see him again.

He needed to work out the shape of his own future, something he hadn't been able to focus on because of his friend. But at the end of the day, he wasn't any closer to deciding how to help Roddy. Perhaps getting him away from the school would help but convincing him when he was on his crusade against Solomons would be difficult. The first step was to talk to him and try and convince him that the new Principal wasn't such a bad guy after all, but first of all, he needed to find him.

*

No sooner had Alexander Stewart left his office, than Bill's mobile rang, it was his solicitor.

'Miles, have you got some good news for me. Has my mother actually seen sense?'

'Good afternoon to you too, Bill. And no, I'm not the bearer of glad tidings, far from it actually.'

'Oh, what is it?'

'The partner here, who specialises in such matters, was approached by Esther's solicitor and let's just say they had a full and frank discussion. First off, your mother will not back down on this. She is adamant she will honour your late father's wishes and is prepared to go to court to do so. Secondly, it is my firm's view that there is no guarantee that we'd be successful in our challenge and the other party knows this as well. So going to court could be a waste of money and the time frame will certainly extend into next year.'

Crabtree paused to see if his client had anything to say. When he didn't, he continued, 'However, Esther does have some sympathy for your situation and she would like to meet with you and Saul to discuss a possible solution. With her solicitor present, I should add. Now before you get too excited, I must point out that it will be nothing like the £2m you were hoping for, so don't get your hopes up.'

'I'm living at the school at the moment, so I haven't been home for a few days. When does she want to meet?'

'As soon as possible. Could you do this week?'

'Saul's coming up on Friday, for a meeting here at the school. We've got a busy day and I don't know when he's heading back to London. We could possibly do first thing say 8.30?'

'If it makes things easier, I'm sure I can arrange for everyone to meet over there, you must have plenty of space.'

'Great idea, that would really help. If that's the case, let's make it 9 o'clock. I'll let Saul know.'

'Good, I'll confirm the arrangements at this end and Bill, as I said, don't get your hopes up.'

*

'The police! What do they want to see me for!' exclaimed Saul.

'They are aware you're involved with Project Waterloo and I assume they're interested in anything you might know about Emile,' said Canning.

'But I never met the guy! This is not good, not good at all.'

'Pull yourself together man,' said Bah, almost shouting. 'You didn't know Emile, so just say that and Waterloo is simply part of you getting to understand one of the bank's current projects. Keep it simple and you'll be fine.'

'They're waiting for you in meeting room two. The man is called Justin Kell. You may have heard of him,' said Canning.

'Can't say I have,' replied Saul.

As he left the room Bah said, 'Remember, where your loyalty lies Saul. You're one of us now and we all have an awful lot at stake.'

Molly had just finished updating Kell when there was a knock on the meeting room door. He didn't know what to make of the fact that Saul Solomons was the brother of the new Head of the Wellington school, other than it wasn't a coincidence. He'd asked Molly to double-check that it wasn't just two random people with the same surname, but she'd just crossed her arms and given him a hard stare.

'You take the lead. I want to focus on how Mr Solomons reacts,' said Kell.

He moved to the far end of the table so he wouldn't be in the interviewee's eyeline.

'Come in,' said Molly.

Saul walked into the room and did a double take when he saw a young woman holding out her hand in welcome and the man sitting at the far end of the table, who clearly wasn't going to say hello.

'Am I in the right place? I thought I was meeting with the police?'

'We are helping the police with this investigation. My name is Molly Cribbs and that's Justin Kell.' She indicated to where her partner was sitting, who acknowledged Saul with a nod of his head.

She sensed Saul relax. Probably because she was not what he was expecting. 'So Saul, could you start by giving me a bit of background on yourself.'

'What do you want to know?'

'Career outline, how you ended up working here.'

'Actually, I don't formally start until 1 September. They've been keeping me appraised of various projects that I'll be involved with when I start. It's a sort of low-key induction process.'

'What does your current employer think of that?'

'To be honest, they don't know. I only come here in the evenings and do any reading they send me at the weekends.'

He was starting to relax, comfortable with the line the young woman was taking.

'You're a very busy man. How did you get the job here?'

'Through an agency, Executive Search. I've been registered with them for years and every now and again they get in touch when an opportunity they think I'll be interested in comes up.'

'You didn't apply for this job then?'

'No, Markita from the agency rang me about a month ago and gave me the brief. It was more money and the bonus scheme sounded better, so I came to see Suzie for an informal chat.'

'The whole process was very quick. When did you get your offer letter and accept the job?'

Molly already knew the answer to this, but she wanted to get a take on his body language when he was answering questions truthfully.

'I think I met with Abebe and the board the following week. and that was when I got offered the job. The written offer came through a couple of days later.'

'Did you know your predecessor, Emile Black?'

Saul's demeanour changed instantly.

'No, I didn't know him. I've never met him, never spoken to him.'

'Why are you speaking of him the past tense?' asked Molly.

'I'm not, I mean I don't know. Look, I do not know the guy.'

'One of the reasons the police asked us to assist them with their enquiries, is because Emile's partner reported him missing and she asked us to look into his disappearance. Did you know he's disappeared?'

'Not really, no. If he has disappeared, it's nothing to do with me!'

'What does not really mean?' asked Molly.

'OK, I'm aware he's gone missing, but it's not my concern. I don't know anything about the guy.'

Molly decided to shift the focus of the interview. 'What's your involvement with Project Waterloo?'

'It's an acquisition that the bank's involved with. With Emile leaving, I'm involved in the regulatory oversight, approvals, etc.'

'Is that allowed, when you haven't been registered with the PRA and FCA?'

'I have an involvement with the work and Francis signs everything off. Anyway, my application has already gone in, I'll be approved for when I officially start next month.'

Saul was starting to sweat and feeling a bit nauseous as he anticipated where the questions were leading. The other concern was it was getting late and he didn't want to miss out on his private table at the casino.

'Will you be involved with the school in any way going forward?'

'Er, I don't think so, maybe. We've not really discussed it.'

Molly nodded and paused the questioning while she made some notes.

'Right, I think that's about it for the time being Saul, thanks for taking the time to speak to us.'

Visibly relieved, Saul stood to leave.

'Actually, I've one more question,' said Molly. 'Don't you think it strange that your brother, William, isn't it, is now the Head of the school your new employer has just bought?'

'It's a coincidence, that's all. Now I really must be going.'

Saul hurried out of the room, slamming the door behind him.

'Nice job,' said Kell. 'Our friend Mr Solomons is a very bad liar. He's up to his neck in this mess and I doubt it will be too long before he cracks.'

21

The briefing Packham had arranged was at the Met's HQ on Victoria Embankment, starting at 10.00 AM. This gave Kell and Molly time to get into the office early and prepare their own briefing notes.

'Got everything you need?' asked Kell.

'Yes, I think so. It'll be exciting to see where I'll be working when I join up with Chris,' Molly replied.

'That reminds me, we must find the time to progress finding your replacement,' said Kell.

'We have been rather busy recently, but you're right. Now they've found Emile's body, I guess our involvement in the case is over, so we should have more time to focus on it.'

'Let's not get ahead of ourselves. The body hasn't been formally identified yet, but sadly I'm sure it's Emile. Uniform have already been to see Zorna, she'll be asked to make the formal ID, subject to the state of the body. Right, we'd better be going. Let's walk down to Tower Hill and get the District line to Embankment.'

They arrived at New Scotland Yard, in plenty of time and it was a good job because the security checks took an age. Eventually, as they sat waiting in a ground-floor reception area, Packham appeared.

'They let you in then,' he joked.

'Aye, very thorough, the only thing they didn't check was my inside leg measurement!'

'Come on, everyone's here. We're on the first floor, so we'll take the stairs. Don't expect any introductions, there's the usual clash of egos with different departments regarding themselves as more important than everyone else.'

'Are you likely to need us on this going forward?' asked Kell.

'The official line will be, thank you very much, the cheque's in the post. But I'll certainly be keeping the lines of communication open. The primary objective is to identify the sources of the criminal activity. Once that's achieved, they may let the bank continue to operate if they think there's more fish to fry. If not, the likelihood is they'll have their regulatory permissions removed. That will be a big deal, as it seldom happens and could create a confidence issue, which the Bank of England will want to avoid.'

Packham led them into a large conference room with a big rectangular table. Two men and two women were seated on opposite sides of the table, clearly seated with their colleagues. There was no acknowledgement as Packham showed them to their seats.

Packham got straight into it. 'This is Justin Kell and Molly Cribbs, who've been assisting with the Emile Black disappearance.'

A couple of nods was the only welcome they got.

The DCI continued, 'Essex Police found the body of a man fitting the general description of Mr Black yesterday afternoon. The body was found at a landfill site, in a pre-incineration storage area. Fortunately, it became exposed as the waste it had been dumped with, was moved closer to the incineration point. One of the employees rang 999. Black's partner, a Miss Zornitsa Elianti is on her way to Essex to identify the body and then an autopsy will take place to confirm the cause of death.'

'Do we know if he was alive when he left the bank?' asked one of the women.

Packham turned to Molly.

'We've spoken to the majority of the staff who were in the office the day Emile handed in his notice. Apart from the receptionist, only three recalled seeing him that morning. I spoke to the security guard who was on duty when the lorry arrived in the service area. He recalls what he describes as a large transit van coming in around lunchtime, to pick up some old servers.

As far as he remembers, the lorry turned around and reversed up to the service lift. He didn't see what was put into the vehicle and doesn't recall anything that may be regarded as suspicious.'

'How long was the vehicle in the service area?'

'The log shows it arriving at 10.52 and leaving at 12.06. This ties in with the CCTV footage.'

Same woman: 'Makes sense. I doubt anyone in the bank would have the wherewithal to do the deed or even give him something to incapacitate him. They used a third party, so that adds another dimension.'

Packham: 'There's still no trace of the van. We've got a number plate, but it's false. The Essex team are still looking, but it could be anywhere with no doubt new plates.'

The man sitting opposite Packham held up his hand. 'The working assumption is that Black was murdered because he was about to blow the whistle on the money laundering his employer was undertaking. To go to such lengths means there must be a lot at stake. If we crack the laundering, we solve the murder simple as that.'

Same woman: 'But it could take some time before we're ready to move on the laundering piece and even then, we might want to let it run to make sure we catch the biggest fishes.'

Packham: 'I propose we let the Essex Major Incident Team handle the murder. And we continue the Streem investigation. Justin, what have you got?'

Before he spoke, Kell looked around the table trying to work out who was who. The woman who had done all the talking was undoubtedly MI6, so that meant the male contributor was probably from the National Crime Agency.

'As I'm sure you're aware the main players in the Exec team at Streem are the CEO Abebe Bah, the FD Francis Hall and the HR Director Suzie Canning. Our view is they are all involved with money laundering and must be aware of what happened to Mr Black.'

'We doubt the HR lady is aware of ML activity,' said the man who hadn't yet spoken.

'I'm surprised the NCA came to that conclusion based on the evidence we've discovered,' replied Kell.

He smiled as noted the obvious discomfort of their department being named and that he'd guessed correctly. He continued, 'Yesterday evening we interviewed Saul Solomons. Saul is Emile Black's replacement and is due to officially start at Streem on 1 September. While he works his notice with his current employer, he is being kept up to date on certain projects that the bank is currently involved with.

One of these is Project Waterloo, which pertains to the purchase of a private school in Hertfordshire, The Wellington. The first red flag regarding Saul's appointment is that it happened so quickly. He was offered the job just a week after Emile Black handed his notice in. Our opinion is that he was specifically targeted by the bank. Molly will explain.'

'Saul was approached by a recruitment agency, Executive Search. He'd been on their books for a number of years and they had introduced him to various job opportunities. The bank has never used this particular agency until Suzie Canning rang them and asked if they had Saul Solomons on their books. We're still not clear how they knew this, but Canning asked them to approach Saul on a financial package that is above the market rate.'

'But why would they want him? Surely there's a big pool of people who'd be appropriate?' asked NCA man.

Kell took over.

'We haven't been able to do a full background check on Saul at this stage, so I suggest that is one of your priorities,' he looked at the guy who'd asked the question, who was tapping away on his tablet.

Before Kell could continue, the woman who first spoke interrupted.

'Mr Kell, it's unusual that you keep referring to this individual by his first name. I'm sure you're aware that the protocol is we use surnames.'

'I am indeed, it's to differentiate between Saul and his brother Bill.' He looked at the confused faces around the table, before continuing. 'The reason why we're certain Ms Canning is involved in the laundering operation is that following the purchase of the Wellington School, Bill

Solomons was promoted to the Principal's position. And Bill is Saul's older brother.'

'Hang on a minute, when did this take place?' MI6 woman asked.

'It completed last week. We don't have access to the financial details of the transaction, but I'm sure you'll agree that a private school is an ideal vehicle for a money laundering operation.' He paused, 'From your reaction, I assume you weren't aware of this?'

To stop the whispered conversations that ensued, Packham stood up.

'Thanks, Justin, Molly, if you could go and wait in my office, please. Alison who's on reception outside will show you.'

Packham's office was on the next floor and once they were settled, Molly asked, 'I don't think they liked you very much Justin, you made them look stupid.'

'It's their own fault. They go around pretending to be all important and they can't even manage basic police work. A classic example of too many cooks. They're supposed to have the bank under close scrutiny and they don't even know about the school deal. It's pathetic.'

Five minutes later Packham appeared. 'You haven't lost your touch then. How to make friends and influence people!'

'Have you left them trying to work out what to do next?'

'After a fashion. The MI6 guys have decided it wasn't their area all along. They don't want to be tainted if the NCA and my team cock it up. So, they'll leave us to it. They only came along today because they want to know what's going on and also because John Bianchi is back in the country.'

'You think Bianchi could be involved with the bank?' asked Molly.

'Yes, I do. It's right up his street, dodgy bank looking for a channel to launder dirty money. We believe he's been trying to drum up business for his cryptocurrency that all that fuss was about in Manchester. But organised crime are playing hardball as it would give him a major stake in the laundering market. That's what MI6 are focussing on, so our paths could cross again before this plays out.'

'What's the next step?' asked Kell.

'We, that is the NCA and my very small team are going to look into the bank deal. Actually, it would be good if we could use Molly for this as she's already very familiar with the case.'

'Makes sense. Does she need to be here?'

'It would certainly help if she was. Are you OK with that, Molly?'

She looked at Justin who nodded his approval.

'OK, but I've got things I need to tidy up with Justin before I start full-time here.'

'It's just the piece around the bank deal. Once that's completed then it's back to the dinosaur , until you come across full-time. OK, Justin?'

'Apart from the dinosaur reference, yes. Is there anything you need me to do?'

'I've been thinking about this. Could you get over to Essex this afternoon for the ID of the body. Zorna was asking if you could be there. I'll clear it with the Head of MIT and ask if you can stay close to their investigation. We mustn't lose sight of the fact that Emile was killed by some ruthless people and we need to find out exactly what happened. Molly, are you OK to work here for the rest of the day?'

Molly nodded, concerned what her boyfriend and boss was getting involved with.

22

After a short debrief with Bah and Canning, where he managed to assure them he hadn't said anything untoward in his interview with Kell, Saul set off to his night on his exclusive table. He tried not to reflect on what he'd got himself into and the potential consequences of working for an employer that paid no heed to rules, regulations or the law, but even with the excitement of the evening ahead, he couldn't shift the feeling that he was becoming enveloped in a dark cloud.

He arrived at Rupert's just after nine and was met by an effusive General Manager. Everything was Mr Solomons this and Mr Solomons that, as he was taken up a flight of stairs to the mezzanine level and shown into a room which had a plate glass window that overlooked the activity of the main ground floor area. The croupier was a smiling young lady who was expertly turning £100 chips in her left hand. There was a stool on either side of the table so he could choose where he sat and stacks of chips on both sides of the wheel.

'I'll leave you in Rosie's very capable hands. We switch the croupiers around every hour unless you'd prefer to maintain continuity, in which case two hours is the maximum we permit. If you need me for anything, just pick up the house phone by the door. OK, all it leaves me to say is good luck and I hope you have a pleasant evening.'

'Good evening, Mr Solomons, I'm Rosie. How many chips would you like to start with? The denominations are £100, £500, £1000, £5000 and £10,000.'

'Let's start with £10k. A mix of £100s and £500s. And please call me, Saul.'

She pushed two stacks of chips in front of him.

'Ready to begin when you are, Saul.'

The first hour was a steady, win some, lose some. Once he'd settled into placing much larger stakes, the routine of bet, spin, win, lose was no different from when he placed much smaller bets. Rosie was replaced just after 10.00 PM by Jacques, who continued the same professional routine.

Just before 11.00 PM he assessed the value of the piles of the chips in front of him and calculated he was slightly up.

'Time I upped the stakes, Jacques, let's swap out these £100s for £1000s.'

'Certainly, sir.'

And the routine began again, but this time it was more bet, spin, lose and Saul started to get agitated.

'Twenty-nine black.' And another loss. He only had a couple of chips in front of him. 'How do I stand, Jacques?'

'Twenty-two thousand four hundred.' He didn't need to say he was down. 'I'll take another ten, thanks,' said Saul.

And the sequence continued.

His mind drifted back to his sixth-form days, playing three-card brag in the common room. It was easy when you played with real money as you could see exactly where you stood. Also, if you got wiped out it was usually only your cigarette and beer money that you lost. This was different.

Despite having nearly £100k in his bank, the magnitude of what he was doing hadn't sunk in and his systematic approach had fogged out the reality of the situation.

He'd stuck with his system all night and was convinced it was just a matter of time before a winning streak would return. The only thing he hadn't introduced, was to increase his bet on red. Instead of doubling up after a loss, his system did allow to increase the stake to three or four times the original. This was only possible if you had a virtually unlimited supply of funds, which of course he now did. Or thought he did.

'I'll take another twenty, thanks, Jacques. Half in ones, half in fives.'

Jacques nodded and pushed the twelve chips in front of him.

Saul looked down at them, taken slightly aback by how few there were.

Finally, he managed, 'Thanks, spin the wheel.'

Two spins later and he was out of chips again. His loss was just short of £45k and he'd only been playing for just over two hours.

At that moment, Jacques got swapped out and Rosie reappeared with the General Manager.

'Can I get you anything, Mr Solomons? Something to eat or drink?'

Realising he hadn't eaten anything since lunchtime, the thought of some food and a cold beer gave him an immediate sense of relief.

'Sure, thanks. I'd like a steak panini and a few chips, thanks. Oh and a couple of bottles of Peroni.'

'I'll organise that straight away. On the house, of course.'

'Of course,' muttered Saul, as he watched the GM hurry out of the room.

He continued playing and had improved his position slightly when the food came. The tray was placed on a table in the corner of the room, with a couple of settees on either side.

Rosie stood silently in her position behind the wheel and watched as he worked his way through the panini and beer. When he'd finished eating, he felt completely exhausted. He'd already decided he wouldn't go to work tomorrow; the interim guy could handle things well enough. But despite the prospect of sleeping as long as he wanted, the itch to continue playing was gone. He felt like his body was a shell. No feelings. No emotion. No energy. He was running on empty.

He stood up. 'I'm done for tonight, thanks, Rosie. But I'll be back tomorrow, in the early afternoon, if that's OK.'

'Certainly, Saul, I'll arrange that for you.'

He pushed his chips back towards her. 'I'll settle up then.'

Rosie smiled. 'Goodnight, Saul.'

He felt refreshed when he woke the following morning. He emailed the office to say he wouldn't be in but was contactable by phone. He'd already told them he wouldn't be in on Friday as he had to get up to the school first thing to meet with Bill and the solicitors and then various meetings throughout the day. He checked his Streem phone for emails and messages and was relieved when there was nothing from them.

On his way home last night, he decided that today would be his last time at the casino. He'd play for a couple of hours, small stakes and whether he was up or down, that would be it. He'd leave at 5.00 PM and that would be that. He needed a break from the gambling and desperately wanted to keep some of his bonus for a holiday, especially if he might need to disappear on the spur of the moment.

This part of his plan sounded quite straightforward. What he was more concerned about was how he could extricate himself from Streem and everything that was going on there. But that was a problem for another day.

He walked into a very quiet Rupert's at just after 2.00 PM. He went to the cashier and asked if he was in the same room as last night.

'You are indeed, Mr Solomons, the table is ready for you.'

He walked up the stairs and headed to the scene of last night's debacle.

He was greeted by the effusive General Manager and was glad to see that Rosie would be looking after him.

Following the usual pleasantries, he sat down and Groundhog Day began again.

During the first hour, his system stood up and was running at a steady £1,000 ahead. This would normally have given him a buzz, but he wasn't making any serious inroads to his negative position with the casino. *Time to shift gears,* he thought, quickly forgetting his original plan for the day.

He been placing no more than £1k at a time so far. £500 on red and £100 on his five preferred numbers. He doubled this to £2k a spin and would start to double up if he lost. It took less than three minutes with a run of five black numbers and his afternoon loss was £64,000. He was over £100k in debt to the casino and his only option was to continue playing.

He was about to ask Rosie for more chips when a voice said, 'I'd quit now if I were you, Saul.'

He spun around and saw a tall, middle-aged man, black hair with flecks of grey at his temples, standing in the doorway.

'You can't come in here This is a private room,' said Saul.

'Actually, I can come in because I own the joint. Also, I'm about to do you a big favour.'

'Who are you? What do you want?'

The man in the smart suit held out his hand. 'I'm John Bianchi and you and I are going to have a serious chat.'

He nodded at Rosie, who dutifully left the room, shutting the door behind her.

'Let's sit down.' He gestured to the seating area where Saul had eaten the previous evening.

'You look familiar. I've seen you somewhere before,' said Saul.

'I was in one of the meetings at the bank. We didn't get introduced. I apologise for that, but things have been a bit hectic since I arrived.'

Saul felt the dark cloud closing in.

'I thought you said you owned this place?'

'I do. Or my organisation does. This and hundreds like it in the States and here in Europe. Being cash businesses, casinos are ideal for our operation.'

Saul was confused. All sorts of questions were flashing around in his mind. Finally, he managed, 'How did you know I was here?'

'Why don't I start at the beginning. The bank you work for Streem is a new client of my organisation. We are a diversified business based in the States, but we have clients all over the world. Before we take on a new business, we do thorough background checks to make sure there is a good, let's call it cultural fit.'

'But why are you here? Why are you bothering me, ruining my day!'

Bianchi laughed. 'I'm not ruining your day at all Saul. In fact, I'm the best thing that's happened to you in a long time.'

There was a moment's silence as Bianchi let what he was saying sink in.

'You've got a gambling problem, Saul. A big one. If we leave it unchecked, you'll ruin not only yourself but also cause problems for your new employer, which means that I have a problem. So, to rectify this I'm going to make a suggestion. You're going to quit gambling altogether. You're not going to place another bet in your life. Understand?'

'Why would I agree to that?'

'Because, my English friend, if you don't, I'll kill you. Is that a good enough reason?'

Saul went white, unable to reply.

'My view is the bank made a mistake when they hired you. They believed your gambling problem would provide a lever to coerce you to do what they wanted. In my experience, this only works up to a point. All addicts are bad news. They can't control their behaviour and they start to do stupid things.'

Saul went to protest, but the American held up his hand.

'The last twenty-four hours proves my point. You've lost over £100k. You have no means to settle your debt, so you think, I know I'll win it back. See what I mean—stupid.'

'Have you been following me?'

Bianchi laughed. 'It's not like the old days in Sicily, there's technology now. It's the phone the bank gave you.

They knew you played here before they hired you, but they follow your every move. And when you own the place it's easy to keep track of your financial position.'

Saul slumped back on the settee and looked up at the ceiling.

'So, here's the deal. I've intervened because there's too much at stake to be risked by a schmuk like you. I've settled your debt here, so now you owe me. That's another reason to do exactly as I say because if you don't.'

Saul finished his sentence, 'You'll kill me.'

'Got it in one. We're going to start washing large sums through the bank in the next few days and you'll make sure all the regulatory checks cover up what's happening. Some of this will go through to the school, out into my digital currency, Mandara and then come back into the bank as clean cash. You keep this running smoothly for the next six months and I'll write off the £100k you owe me.

Also, it's my opinion we need your brother fully on board with what's going on, to avoid any surprises down the road. You need to convince him and quickly. Got it?'

'Yes, understood. But what about the £2m we have to find? Can you help with that?'

Bianchi's steel blue eyes stared him down.

'Absolutely, not. That's down to you and your bro. Now, I'm getting hungry. Let's go and get something to eat and we can continue our cosy little chat.'

23

Kell met Emile Black's girlfriend at the police station in Chelmsford. Zorna Elianti was sitting in an interview room with her hands resting gently on the table. She smiled as Kell was let in but didn't stand to greet him.

'Hello, Zorna. I won't ask how you're doing as I know this must be terrible for you. What have the police said?'

She looked at him with tears running down her face.

'They believe the body they found is Emile. He didn't have any ID on him, but the description matches. Now, you're here I assume they'll take us to do the identification.'

'That'll be in the coroner's office. In view of the circumstances, an autopsy will have already been performed. It should tell us how Emile died.' He didn't see any point in putting any doubt into her mind that it would be Emile's body.

'I'll speak to the detective in charge. Would you like to know the details?'

'Yes, I think I would.'

He didn't have anything more to say, so they sat in silence until the DCI running the investigation came in ten minutes later.

'Miss Elianti, Mr Kell. DCI Vernon Sams. Apologies for being late. I've been updating the Chief Super, who sends his apologies he can't be here himself.'

Zorna simply nodded. Kell said, 'Please call me Justin.'

'Right, of course. Everything is ready for you. The coroner's office is in the adjacent building. Please follow me.'

Kell had a long list of questions he wanted to ask but decided to wait until after Zorna had identified the body. He'd wanted to meet with the DCI separately so as not to upset her.

They were shown into the viewing area and stood in front of a large plate glass window. Sams spoke into an intercom and a gurney was wheeled to in front of them, covered with a green hospital sheet.

'Are you ready?' asked the detective.

Zorna nodded and the sheet was pulled back to show the face of Emile Black.

'He looks so peaceful,' she said.

'Zorna. I need you to confirm it's Emile,' said Sams.

'Yes, it's my darling, Emile. Now please can I have a few minutes on my own.'

As soon as they were out of the room Kell asked, 'Have you got time to bring me up to date?'

'Sure, do you fancy a coffee? It's not very good, but I guess you've had your fair share.' When they settled in the police canteen, Kell got straight to the point. 'How did he die.'

'Let me take it back a stage. The autopsy showed that he was drugged. The amount of ketamine and propofol in his system suggests this would have been administered around the time he was at the bank. The fact that he was unconscious when he was put in the van makes sense. It's unlikely he would have got in voluntarily.'

'How would it have been administered?'

'It was injected. There is a recent hypodermic mark on his neck. But, before you say anything, there were also traces of flunitrazepam, better known as Rohypnol, in his system. Our assumption is this was probably in a drink like tea or coffee. It would have made him very drowsy and not aware of the injection.'

'So, someone in the bank must have dosed his coffee and potentially applied the injection.'

'Certainly, for the Rohypnol. Depending on how much they gave him, they could have gotten him into the van. It disappears from the system quickly, so it's impossible to be certain. All we can say for definite is that the injection that killed him was given either at the bank or in the van.'

'How did you find the body?'

'A phone call from the waste disposal site. It was anonymous and from a burner, so nothing we can trace. It was a 999 call, which simply said, 'Dead body at Sharwell Green.' No distinctive accent, less than two seconds, but maybe someone has a conscience. It was in a huge pile about to be incinerated. An hour or so later and we'd never have found Emile Black.'

A young policewoman came across to their table. 'Sorry to interrupt, sir, Miss Elianti would like to go home.'

'Thanks. Have you got enough for now?' asked Sams.

'Yes, you've been very helpful. Can I hitch a ride back with Zorna?'

'Of course and I'll keep you posted of any developments.'

They were driven back to London in an unmarked police car without a word being spoken. They dropped Zorna off at her flat.

'Thanks for everything you've done, Justin. Please let me know when you find out who killed him. I don't want to read about in the press.'

'Molly or I will keep in touch. If there's anything you need, just call.' She nodded and got out of the car to try to face the rest of her life.

'Where would you like me to take you, sir?' asked the driver.

Kell checked his watch. It was 6.45 PM.

'I need to go back to the office, so Brick Lane please.'

*

Saul was up early on Friday morning and despite everything that had happened in the last 48 hours he felt surprisingly calm about the day ahead. His dinner with Bianchi had lasted well into the evening. He'd learned all about how his digital currency Mandara operated and the vast scale of the operation.

The American portrayed himself as being a completely legitimate businessman, although it was clear he didn't ask any questions as to where his clients' money came from. He suspected this was only a very small part of his story, but Bianchi was very clear that he couldn't help him and his brother with finding the £2m they needed. He had however made a suggestion that Saul thought might be acceptable to his mother and solve the problem.

He'd decided that he'd stay over with Bill this evening as he wanted to explain everything about what was going on at the bank and Bianchi's involvement in detail. He needed his brother to be on precisely the same page, so they could see this through together. He wasn't sure it was brotherly love at this stage, but he'd got closer to Bill in recent weeks and if things worked out, then maybe they could enjoy spending more time together.

He pulled into the school at just after 8 o'clock and made his way to his brother's office. He walked in to find his brother in an animated conversation with their solicitor, Miles Crabtree.

'Isn't he supposed to be the bloody expert?' said Bill.

'Look, just calm down, Bill. I'll say it again. There is no guarantee you'll win the case. You've seen his written opinion. Whilst the grounds are legitimate, the balance of probability is we'll lose. Esther's solicitors are aware of this and it's a professional courtesy that they're meeting us this morning, so we can all hear what your mother has to say. One way or another, I strongly recommend that this ends today.'

'Morning Miles, Bill. I gather our expert probate lawyer has given us up as a bad job,' said Saul.

Crabtree sighed, 'It's not like that. But going to court would be expensive for you and disastrous PR for our firm. So, let's see what your mother's got to say and put this to bed.'

There was a knock on the open office door and Bill's secretary appeared. 'Mrs Solomons is here, with a gentleman. I've put them in the Windsor Room and served them coffee.'

'Thanks, we'll be right there.' Bill stood up and stormed out of the room muttering to himself. Saul looked at Crabtree who said, 'This shouldn't take too long.'

Following the introductions and pleasantries, Esther's solicitor Julian Stibson suggested he begin.

'Firstly, Mrs Solomons has come here this morning in good faith. This matter is causing her a great deal of stress and I'm sure you'll agree, we'd all like it resolved amicably.'

Esther sat stony-faced, looking down at the table.

'Miles, we've spoken with your firm and I believe we are agreed that whilst there are legitimate grounds to contest the Will, proceeding to court would be an unnecessary and expensive waste of time for all concerned. Mrs Solomons has religiously ensured that her late husband's wishes have been executed to the letter, but does appreciate the frustration of William and Saul, that their father did not include any settlement for them.'

He paused and took a sip of his coffee.

'Throughout her life, your mother has acquired funds of her own from various investments, that my firm have administered on her behalf. These are completely separate from your late father's estate and therefore not restricted by the terms of his Will. It is from these funds that she is offering to give £100,000 each to William and Saul.

Whilst this is not the £2m that is sought, she hopes that the gesture will help to finalise this matter. I've taken the liberty to draw up the appropriate papers for inheritance tax purposes, which I will leave for your consideration.'

There was silence while they waited to see if he'd finished.

Saul looked at his brother but couldn't catch his eye. He'd wanted to discuss his idea with him before the meeting, but decided it was now or never.

'Thank you, mother. A very generous offer, which we appreciate but which sadly doesn't help us with our investment opportunity. We were wondering whether you'd consider loaning us the money. We'd agree an appropriate rate of interest, for the remainder of your life, although we'd expect to repay it in the next few years. This means the money is still "yours" and we are able to complete our investment.'

Esther spoke for the first time. 'I assume you're saying that this is the investment in the school. How on earth will that generate £2m over the next few years? It's preposterous.'

Julian Stibson got in just before Bill was about to erupt.

'Thank you, Saul, for your suggestion. My firm hasn't seen the details of this investment and before we advise your mother, we'd need to see the full details.'

He put his hand on his client's arm, as Esther clearly had something she wanted to say.

'I'm sure my clients would be prepared to do this, but only if Mrs Solomons is genuinely prepared to consider it,' said Crabtree.

Esther had regained her composure. 'I'm going to the Eastbourne house later this afternoon. I'll be back this time next week. I'll give you my answer then.'

'Is that acceptable?' Stibson asked.

'I suppose it'll have to be,' said Bill, who stormed out of the room without another word.

Saul walked round the table to his mother and gave her a hug.

'I'm sorry about all this. Thanks for the offer of your money and also for agreeing to think about what I've proposed. Have a lovely time in Eastbourne.'

Saul found his brother pacing around his office. 'I'm sorry I didn't get the chance to discuss my proposal with you before the meeting, but at least it gives us an option to raise the £2m.'

'That's not the point. Why should we have to borrow what's rightfully ours! We could end up paying her interest on our own money. It doesn't make sense and it's simply not fair.'

'Look, I had a long chat with John Bianchi the other evening and I don't think we need to worry about being able to fund the interest payments or even pay the full £2m back in relatively short order. There are plans to buy other schools like Wellington and really scale up the model. You and I are integral to their plans, so let's see what she's got to say when she gets back from Eastbourne.'

'Maybe you're right, but it doesn't matter. I've got an idea of my own. It's our money and I fully intend to get it.'

24

The days of the week didn't usually matter to Roddy Roan. Even in term time he'd never consciously think whether it was a Tuesday or a Friday, he'd simply let his friends tell him which class was next and follow them there.

During the holidays he drifted from one day to the next, oblivious to what day it was. Until now. He'd decided his campaign against Solomons needed a defining moment. Something on a grand scale. His problem was the different religions had their Holy Day on different days of the week. Most typically a Friday, Saturday or a Sunday, but which day to choose for his grand act?

He'd now dismissed his idea about following the plagues of Egypt from the Old Testament, although there was one story from Exodus that had captured his imagination. So, to avoid any claims of religious fanaticism, he planned his grand finale to start late on Friday evening so that Solomons and his God would have a memorable Sabbath. With his planning complete, Solomons would get what he deserved.

*

By the time the Board meeting finished at just after 6.00 PM, Saul and Bill were exhausted. Following the fractious meeting with their mother that morning, it was meeting after meeting, most of which focussed on the financials to provide the front for the processing of the dirty money from Streem.

Saul was surprised at how easily his brother had accepted the criminal activity he was now embroiled with. He could see why Bah had targeted him to be the Principal. He knew the workings of the school inside out. He brought a realism to the growth in pupil numbers; what new parents would value in a private school; their tolerance to pay what he thought were ridiculously high fees and the type of teachers that needed to be recruited. And not once did he question where the money came from or how much would wash through the books each month.

'That was one tough day, Bill. I'm shattered. Do you fancy grabbing a beer or two?'

'Yeh, you're right. I don't see why we need so many different models for the funding and all that. My head's spinning with numbers.'

'We are very thorough. It's important that nothing looks out of the ordinary. We need the perfect façade for the outside world. Anyway, enough of work for one day. How about we head down to the Bell for a couple? It's a lovely evening and they've plenty of outside tables.'

'Sure, but you'll have to drive. My car is still sitting on the drive at the house. I haven't had a chance to get the AA out to look at it.'

'No problem. We'll only have a couple. We could go back there later if you fancy. Mother's gone to Eastbourne, so we'll have the place to ourselves?'

'Good idea, but I've got three lots of parents coming first thing in the morning to show around, so it's easier if I stay here. You can go back if you want, but I've sorted a decent room for you in the staff wing.'

'OK, it is slightly quicker to get back to London from here. Come on, let's go and don't forget to bring your wallet!'

They settled at an outside table in the warm evening sunshine. They hadn't spoken much on the ten-minute drive and the silence continued as they sipped their drinks, until Saul blurted out.

'I've a gambling problem. It's been going on for years and I desperately need to do something about it.'

His brother looked incredulous. 'What. What did you say?'

For the next half an hour, Saul told his brother an abridged version of his fall into gambling. From the days when he was in the sixth form, playing cards with his friends, through his fascination with fruit machines, before discovering the roulette wheel. He omitted how he'd been forced to ask their mother for handouts on numerous occasions, using the cover of waiting for an investment to come good. But as that slate was now clean, he didn't see the need to include it.

When it appeared he'd finished, Bill asked, 'Have you sought any help?'

'No, but I know I should. I always thought, still do in fact, that I can control it. But I get this urge, this itch that constantly needs to be scratched.' He shaked his head. 'And that's not all. Have you been introduced to John Bianchi yet?'

'No. He hasn't been to the school, but his name has come up a few times. Why, who is he?'

'I'm not actually sure. I had a long discussion with him the other evening, which is the final bit of my story that I need to tell you. You know I think the bank targeted me, not just because they wanted the school and you to run it, but they also know about my gambling.

Right from the start, they've dangled money in front of me, paid me a joining bonus, then another one when you said you'd take the Head's job. They knew about my gambling and I played into their hands when I lost the bloody lot. The other afternoon, just as I'd hit rock bottom again with just a few pounds in front of me, Bianchi appears at my private table. He said he owned the place, Rupert's and that he'd take care of my debt. It appears he owns or rather his organisation owns all sorts of businesses in the States and here in London.

This includes a cryptocurrency, a digital currency like Bitcoin. This is how they move illicit money through the financial system under the radar of the authorities. My view is he's calling most of the shots as far as the bank are concerned and he made it very clear that I had to stick around and fudge all the regulatory checks.'

'Will he help with the £2m we need?'

Saul laughed. 'No, he won't. I'll be suitably rewarded for my part in this illegal enterprise, but he made it clear that the two mill is down to us. Oh and just to be clear, if I get caught then I'm going to prison.'

'This is a bloody mess. What with mother and now this. Christ, Saul, what are we going to do?'

'I'm running out of ideas, but you said you had something you could do.'

'Never, mind that, let's just say I'm going to do everything to protect our situation. Anyway, come on let's get back. I'll show you your room, there's no point in you going back to the house tonight.'

'How very, assertive of you, big brother.'

And with that, they left.

*

Kell got back to the office on Brick Lane to find Molly at her desk staring intently at her laptop. He slung his backpack on his chair and they embraced in the middle of the room.

'I didn't expect to find you here at this hour?' he said.

'I know you too well Justin Kell. I knew you'd come back in to type up your notes and check if there were any new developments. Anyway, I couldn't work in that place. They wouldn't give remote access to our servers here, so there wasn't much that I could do. I got back here about three and have been waiting ever since.'

'Have you found much about the activities at Streem?'

Molly returned to her desk.

'Have a look at this. Chris sent me this file which shows a comparison of the money flowing into and out of the bank since it became regulated. Each year is represented by a different colour. You can discount year one as it's not a full year as they're in start-up mode. But from year two and year three you can start to see a trend developing.'

Kell studied the screen. 'OK, the numbers increase year on year, but you'd expect that wouldn't you?'

'You would. Until you overlay the figures from the returns they have to make to the regulator.'

She clicked on a couple of keys and new lines appeared on the screen.

'I see what you mean. There's a growing disparity for the three years they've been operating. In fact, their standard trading looks pretty static, it's the other stuff that's increasing. How do Chris's team know about the dirty money? How can they distinguish between what's clean and what isn't?'

'It's complicated, but basically down to all the monitoring they do. Some of it is assumptive, but it's all about tracking back to the source.' She turned to look at him.

'It's the type of thing I'll be doing when I join his team. The thing is darling, it's really boring. I'll be staring at a screen all day. It won't be like working here, where each day is different. I'm not sure I want to do it.'

He put his arms around her. 'I know, I know. Let's have a chat with Chris when this case is over. I'm sure he'll understand if you decide to change your mind.'

'But will he? I've signed the contract and the money is really good. I don't know what's best for me, for us, for everything.'

She was fighting to hold back her tears.

'Look, we'll work this out together. But for now, let's focus on our involvement with the bank and Emile's death. It was his body by the way and things aren't looking good for Suzie Canning.'

'Why just her and not the others?' asked Molly.

'We know it's Emile and now there is a strong possibility that he was murdered at the bank, it's become a crime scene. The Essex MIT and the Met are probably already there securing the site and as we know Ms Canning was the last person to see Emile alive.'

'But it was four weeks ago? Will there still be any evidence lying around?'

'Now, the forensic teams are involved, they'll probably focus on any traces of the drugs that were used to sedate Emile or to kill him. The main players will now be interviewed by the police, so it's not the best PR for the bank.'

'So, I guess that means that as far as we're concerned the case is over,' said Molly.

'Not necessarily. We've gathered a lot of evidence from our dealings with Canning and Bah and of course, our interviews with the staff who were there that day. We'll need to hand this over to them as soon as possible, probably Monday, so it's going to be a working weekend.'

She smiled at him. 'So long as I'm working with you, I'm happy.'

He took her in his arms. 'Look, we'll make sure we find the time to discuss your job offer and everything that goes with it. Whatever you decide, you'll have my full support. Now, it's late, so let's head home and have any early night. We've a busy couple of days ahead.'

*

Roddy stood stock still, his arms spread and his head raised to look at the heavens. He stared as the flames rose high into the clear, starry night. He was in awe of what was happening. It was a sign from the Gods that he had chosen the right path.

His torment of the last six years was being washed away, not by the cleansing of water, but the purification of fire. He sank to his knees and screamed a prayer of thanks to all the gods of all the religions. He felt blessed. He felt divine. In the distance, he heard sirens and knew it was time for him to leave. He turned his back on the inferno and began the long walk back to the school.

25

Al was starting to get concerned. He'd been looking for his friend all afternoon, but he wasn't in any of his usual haunts and no one had seen him. Eventually, he gave up and went to the refectory to get something to eat. There were a couple of tables occupied by the familiar faces of the summer boarders, but he decided to sit on his own and do some thinking.

The large clock on the wall showed it was seven-thirty. The staff had started tidying up and he was fortunate to get the last couple of pieces of pizza and a few lukewarm chips. He sat down at the nearest table, eating on autopilot as he tried to think where Roddy might be.

His mind wandered back to their first year at the school. The four of them were decent horse riders, the product of a privileged upbringing, playing on junior polo teams. It was Roddy who had christened them "The Four Horsemen" and the name had stuck even when they stopped playing the following year because they'd decided it wasn't macho enough.

Roddy had had a problem with Solomons from day one. He'd been the most rebellious of their little gang, but for some reason, he'd hated Solomons from the first English lesson when they'd gotten into an argument of the merits of

Shakespeare. Roddy had always been passionate about Milton and Webster whose tales and epic poetry told, in his mind, real stories of religious persecution and death. Shakespeare was childish in comparison, with little more than myth and fairy tales of sprites and fairies.

Unfortunately, Solomons took the bait and his condescending attitude only inflamed Roddy more until it became an intellectual boxing match, with the two protagonists desperate to have the last word.

Solomons didn't cover himself in glory that day and Roddy's crusade against the teacher slowly sucked them all in. He personally had never had any trouble with the guy, but Roddy's vitriol was infectious and by year 9, they were all an integral part of the stupid pranks that their friend dreamed up.

However, it was only in the last twelve months that Roddy's mental state began to give him cause for concern. His fascination with religion became an obsession. In his own time, he started to study the different faiths from around the world, which gave him more reason for obtuse discussion not just with his friends but also in class with Solomons. Sometimes whole lessons would be lost as they argued back and forth, debating comparisons and contradictions in the various scriptures.

Now, he'd gone missing and Al had a feeling in his gut that something bad, really bad was about to happen.

He continued his search around the school grounds until it was fully dark. Exhausted he went back to their dorm, slumped into bed and fell into a deep sleep.

'Al, Al, wake up. Al, it's a miracle, it's happened. Al, it's an act of God. Hallelujah, it's done!'

He awoke in a start and sat up in semi-shock to see Roddy standing at the foot of his bed, with his rucksack slung over his shoulder. He switched on his bedside lamp and watched as his friend sank to his knees in prayer.

'Oh no, Roddy, what have you done?'

*

On the other side of the school, Bill Solomons was also woken up. Not by somebody coming into his room, but by the ringing of his mobile phone. Since finally getting into bed, he'd tossed and turned struggling to find sleep as his mind wouldn't stop trying to process everything that was going on.

'Hello.'

'Mr Solomons?'

'Yes, Bill Solomons speaking, who's this?'

'Mr Solomons, I'm Fire Chief Davis. I'm afraid I've got some bad news. There's been a fire at your house.'

'A fire, oh my god. Is it bad?'

Ignoring the question, the Fire Chief continued, 'Do you know if anyone was in the house this evening. There isn't a contact number for Mrs Solomons, who I understand is the registered owner.'

'Er, no, I don't think so. Mother went down to her house in Eastbourne this afternoon, so the house was empty.' He paused, 'Unless, oh no, Saul. Look I'm coming straight over.'

He ended the call, pulled on his jogging bottoms and ran down the corridor to where he hoped Saul was sleeping. He barged into the room and a split second later, his startled brother sat up.

'Christ, Bill, what are doing! You could have given me a heart attack!'

'There's been a fire at the house. Come on we need to get over there.'

Five minutes later, they were in the staff car park. Bill hurried over to a dark Renault saloon, unlocking the doors with remote key.

'Whose car is this? I thought you said yours was out of action at the house?'

'I decided I needed to lease one, while the Ford is out of action. There's lots of running around that I need to do.'

Saul looked at his brother as they sped out of the school grounds. It was 3.30 AM on what was going to be a very long day.

They could see the red glow above the tree line as soon as they turned out of the entrance onto the small B Road. By road, it was six miles from their family home to the Wellington School. With no traffic, it took them under ten minutes to complete the journey. There was a solitary police car parked across the end of the drive.

Once the PC was happy they were who they said they were, they drove down the driveway before they were stopped again, fifty yards short of the large circular driveway that curved up to the front door. They got out and stared in disbelief at what they saw. The whole house was ablaze. Four fire engines and their teams were battling the blaze.

'Thank goodness, you and mother weren't home,' said Saul.

'Yes, thank goodness,' muttered his brother.

Two men walked towards them from a police car that was parked on the other side of the driveway, next to Bill's old Ford Mondeo.

'Mr Solomons? I'm Fire Chief Davis, we spoke on the phone. This is DS Wilcox.'

'Yes, I'm Bill Solomons and this is my brother Saul.'

The DS asked. 'Who lives in the house?'

'I live there with our mother,' replied Bill.

'You told the Chief that Mrs Solomons is away in Eastbourne at the moment. Do you have a number you can contact her on?'

'She doesn't have a mobile, but we have the landline number.' Saul got out his phone, scrolled through his contacts, tapped on the number for the Eastbourne house and let it ring for a minute before stating the obvious. 'No answer, there's only one phone and it's downstairs. She wouldn't be able to hear it ring from her bedroom.'

The DS nodded. 'OK, what's the address. I'll get the locals to go and check she's there.'

'There's no reason she wouldn't be. She left at lunchtime and it only takes a couple of hours,' said Bill.

'Just routine stuff, we need to do. I'm sure you understand. It'll be a big shock for her. Can one of you get down there to be with her?'

They looked at each other, Bill shaking his head. 'I'm showing some parents around the school later this morning. Saul, what about you?'

'Yes, I can head down there later, but first off. What happened here. How did the fire start?'

The Fire Chief answered, 'We won't know until the forensic guys can get in. It's an old house with a wooden structure and I'm guessing a lot of old furniture that isn't as fire-resistant as the modern stuff. But it's pointless speculating until we can get in.'

'When will that be?' asked Bill.

'We should have the fire out, later today. We then need to damp it down to make sure there's no chance of any reignition. So, possibly tomorrow but more likely Monday.'

'Are you alright, Mr Solomons, you don't look very well?' the DS asked.

Bill was sweating heavily and his whole body had started to shake.

'Come and sit down in the squad car. It must be a big shock to see your home burning down.'

The DS led Bill away, leaving Saul with the Fire Chief.

'He's not particularly friendly, is he?' said Saul.

The Chief looked at him. 'The thing is with policemen, that they always think the worst. Not like my guys, we have to be positive and optimistic or the job would drive us mad.'

'What do you mean?'

'Guess what the first question DS Wilcox asked me when he got here.'

'No idea,' said a perplexed Saul.

'Do you think it's arson? That's what he asked.'

'Arson! But who would want to burn our family home down?'

'In my experience, there's always someone. But we leave that to the police. Now excuse me, I need to get back to my team.'

26

Kell and Molly worked through the weekend, typing up the notes of all the interviews with the bank staff, identifying inconsistencies and areas that needed further investigation. It was a comprehensive report that Kell emailed to Packham on Sunday evening.

'Right, now we've boxed that off, how about talking over Chris's job offer with a glass of wine,' said Kell.

'Sounds good to me. White or red?'

'White, please. There should be a bottle of sauvignon in the fridge.'

Molly got the wine and they snuggled up on the sofa, slowly sipping their drinks.

'So, what's troubling you about this job. I thought it was everything you've been hoping for.'

Molly put her glass on the coffee table.

'When I was there the other day, I spent an hour with one the "technicals" as they're called. She showed me two of the systems they use and how they can follow money going through the financial system. It's straightforward to use unless you hit a "blind spot". That can be interesting because then the challenge is how to open up that area and so you refer to the IT guys to include it in the framework. The problem is you don't speak to anyone. There wasn't even any banter between the team who've been working together for the last six months!'

'It does sound grim, staring at a screen all day, but that's what work is for a lot of people these days.'

'I know, but that doesn't mean it'll work for me. Honestly, I don't think I can do it. It would drive me mad. And then I'd be coming home all grumpy and hearing about your glamorous life as a PI!'

'You know it's not always like that. There's a lot of drudgery in our work too.'

'I know, but at least I get to speak to people. Seriously, Justin, I can't do it. I'll ring Chris tomorrow and tell him.'

'OK, if that's what you want, you've got my full support. We still need to take someone on, so now we've finished with this case, we must make the time to find the right person.'

They were interrupted by a ping on his phone.

'It's Chris saying thanks for our report and can we make a briefing at HQ at nine in the morning. Apparently, there's been a development.'

'That's early, perhaps we'd better have an early night then.' She smiled. 'And let's take the bottle of wine with us.'

The tube was rammed as usual as they made their way across town to Embankment. By the time they'd got through the security checks, it was already 9.00 AM. Packham was waiting for them, looking more harassed than usual.

'Don't worry, we're running late. It's kicking off big time. Come on, we can have a coffee in my office, while they try and decide who is responsible for what.'

Packham's office was a mess. His desk was covered in files, with more on the floor.

'I thought everything was digital these days. What happened to paperless policing?' asked Kell.

'Don't go there. Now, assume it's coffee for you, Justin. Peppermint tea, Molly?' They nodded and Packham stuck his head out of the door and shouted in the order.

'So, what's the big development, that's got everyone in such a frenzy?' asked Kell.

'In the early hours of Saturday morning, there was a fire at a house just outside a small village in Hertfordshire. About ten miles from St Albans. It was an old building, lots of wood and was finally put out on Saturday afternoon. The forensic team were finally given the all-clear to go in yesterday lunchtime and establish the cause. Initially, it was believed that neither of the usual occupants were in the building at the time, however, the body of a woman was discovered, together with signs that the fire was started deliberately.'

Kell and Molly looked at each other trying to understand what all this had to do with them.

'The house belonged to Esther Solomons. She lived there with her eldest son William. Until the body can be identified by dental records, the working assumption is the body is that of Esther Solomons and we're dealing with a murder.'

*

Saul tried ringing the Eastbourne house again, just before he set off on the two-and-a-half hour drive down to the coast and again, his mother didn't answer. For some reason, he didn't have any overwhelming emotions at seeing the family home burn down. Probably because he hadn't lived there for such a long time.

He was also thinking how this might just play into their hands with regard to getting the money they needed. He thought that Bill had a share in the house. It wasn't a 50/50 split with mother, but because he lived there the ownership had been formalised in some way. This would mean his brother would be entitled to part of whatever the insurance paid out, which could go towards the funds they needed.

The traffic was quiet at such an early hour on a Saturday. Even the M25 wasn't busy. He'd only been to the Eastbourne house a handful of times, but as it was right on the front, with a wonderful sea view, he had no trouble driving straight there, pulling up just after 7.00 AM.

He parked on the short driveway and before he'd opened his door to get out, a frantic Mrs Buckle was hurrying down the drive.

'Oh Saul, I'm so glad you're here. What's the matter with her? Has she been taken ill?' Saul didn't understand what she was saying.

'I'm sorry. I'm here to see mother.'

They stood looking at each other, in stunned silence.

'She is here, isn't she?'

The housekeeper started to cry. 'No, she isn't. Is she still at home?'

Saul's heart sank as he tried to maintain his composure. 'Come on, let's get the kettle on. I'll tell you all about it.'

Over a steaming hot cup of tea, Saul ran through the story of the fire.

'So you see, I came down straight away to tell her the news. But if she's not here, then—'

Bill sat in the front of the police car with the DS. He was slowly regaining his composure and his breathing was returning to normal. The policeman didn't waste any time. 'Where are you staying at the moment if you're not at home?'

'I'm the Principal of the Wellington school. I've my own room there, so I can stay over when I'm working late.'

'Were you working late last night then? I thought you'd be quiet, with it being the summer holidays.'

'The school was recently sold, so there are new owners. I was asked to take over as the Head to maintain continuity. I'm finding it quite challenging as its enrolment time and there's a big push to increase student numbers. I've been staying there for the last week or so. It's much more convenient.'

'How long have you and your mother lived here?'

'It's been the family home for nearly forty years. Father bought it about the time I was born. I've lived here most of life apart from when I was Uni and a couple of ill-fated relationships. I moved back in, must have been seven years ago.'

The policeman let the silence stretch as he made his notes, before asking, 'What's it like to be living with your mum at your age?'

'I know it seems odd, but it's not like that. I have the east wing of the house. It's a bit grand to call it a wing, but mother does. She lives in the larger western part. We occasionally have dinner together but that's it. It's like I've got a place of my own.'

'And your dad?'

'He died last year. Now, unless there's anything else, I should get back to the school. I've lots to do.'

'Just one more question, Mr Solomons. Whose car is that?' He gestured to the car parked next to them.

'Oh, that's mine. It wouldn't start the other morning and I haven't had a chance to get the AA out. Another reason why I was staying at school.'

'OK, that's all for now. I'm sorry about the loss of your home. You'll need to provide a formal statement next week once the fire crew has finished up and forensics have established the cause. I'll come to the school if I need anything in the meantime.'

Al looked at the dishevelled mess of his friend. He stank of smoke and his long hair was matted to his head with bits of foliage stuck here and there. He really did look like he'd been dragged through a hedge backwards.

'Come on, let's get you cleaned up and then you need to get some sleep. We'll talk later.'

Roddy showered and put clean clothes on. He'd dumped what he had been wearing in the laundry bag. When he appeared back in the dorm, he looked calm and lucid. He didn't look particularly tired, considering he'd been up all night.

'Do you want to get some sleep or shall we do something we've never done before and be the first into Saturday breakfast?' asked Al.

'Mmmm, breakfast, I think. I'm actually rather hungry. And I've got so much news to tell you Alexander, so much news.'

They headed off to the refectory with Al dreading what his friend was going to tell him.

27

It was pure adrenalin that got him through showing the parents and their aspiring children around the school. He'd done it so many times recently that he was on autopilot with the spiel and it helped they always asked the same predictable questions.

Two of the three were happy to enrol there and then, whilst the third had one more establishment to see later that day. It was lunchtime when they'd all left and he could return to his office to take stock of last night's events. It was clear the house was gone. The insurance would pay to have it rebuilt, but he was hoping he'd be able to get some money out of it. It was just a matter of time and a case of waiting for the inevitable.

He startled when his mobile rang and was only slightly relieved when he saw it was his brother.

'Hi, Saul, how did she take the news?'

'She's not here, Bill. Mrs B came down yesterday morning to get the place ready. She was expecting mother mid-afternoon, teatime at the latest.'

'What do you mean, she's not there. Has there been an accident? Have you spoken to that taxi service she uses?'

'No, not yet. I haven't got their number. Mrs Buckle says it's in the phone book in the hall, which clearly doesn't help much and she can't remember the name. Look, I'm heading back shortly. Mrs B is going to stay in case mother shows up. I'll meet you at the school. Text me the number of the policeman, the sergeant we were speaking to. We need to let him know she's not here.'

'Wilcox. I'll send it now. See you later.'

Saul looked at his phone, surprised by the abrupt ending to the call. His brother sounded distracted, although that was to be expected when his home had just burned down. He said goodbye to Mrs Buckle and set off back to Hertfordshire.

He didn't have a hands-free device, so he dialled the policeman's number and put his phone on speaker. It went straight to voicemail. He left a message saying their mother wasn't in Eastbourne. For the whole journey, he had just one unimaginable thought in his head. She couldn't have been, could she?

He found Bill in his office, working on his laptop.

'Any news?' he asked.

His brother looked up and he could see the sheer exhaustion on his face.

'Nothing.' Was all he could manage in reply.

'I didn't get to speak to Wilcox, just left him a message.' He looked at his brother who had turned back to his screen.

'Bill, what's going on? You're acting like nothing's happened. Have you tried getting in touch with her friends? Is the fire out yet? When will they be able to find out what happened? Our mother is missing and you're just sitting here, doing nothing!'

'No need to shout, Saul. The thing is I have this horrible feeling, that, you know, she is probably in the house. I think she's dead, Saul.'

'So how can you just be sitting here! I'm going back to the house to see what I can find out. You coming or not?'

'You go. I can't face it at the moment. I'll be here when you get back.'

'Unbelievable!' Saul stormed out.

The policeman at the end of the drive was reluctant to let him through until he finally convinced him he was a family member and needed to speak to DS Wilcox.

'The DS left a while ago, but one of the DCs will still be here.'

Saul parked in the same spot as last night. As soon as he was out of the car, he was approached by a man of similar age to himself, dressed in a shabby suit with his tie tied loosely around his neck.

'DC Shaw. You must be Mr Solomons. Is it Saul or William?'

'It's Saul. Pleased to meet you.'

'The DS has gone back to the station. There's not much for us to do until the forensic team has been in and established the cause. I've no more news I'm afraid.'

'I left him a message. Do you know if he got it?'

'He hasn't passed anything on to me. Is it important?'

'Yes, very. Our mother isn't at her Eastbourne house. I've just driven there and back and she's not there. Her housekeeper is still there and she'll ring me if she turns up.'

He turned and looked at the smouldering house.

'I see. Is there anywhere else she could be, any friends she could be staying with?'

'We don't have any contact numbers. Mother was quite old-fashioned. No mobile phone, no tablet. Everything was written down in her diary or the phone book. When will the forensic guys be able to go in?'

'They're lined up for tomorrow, subject to the fire chief giving the OK. Look, there's nothing more you can do here. We'll ring you if there are any developments. Go home and get some sleep, you look like you could use it.'

*

Al watched as his friend tucked into his bacon and eggs as though he hadn't eaten for a week. Once that was finished, he started on the mound of toast he'd piled onto his plate. When he'd decided he'd had enough, he sat back and smiled at his friend.

'That was the best breakfast I've ever had!'

Al waited to see if he'd say anything else, but the dazed look quickly returned, with Roddy staring at nothing in particular.

'So where did you get to last night? Was there a bonfire somewhere, you stank of smoke when you got in?'

'Yes, a bonfire that was it. The flames were huge. A real spectacle.'

'And who was at this bonfire?'

Roddy paused before his eyes returned to sharp focus. 'Why me and Mr Solomons, of course.'

'You mean Doc Solomons? Why was he at a bonfire and why were you with him? Come on, Rod, you're not making sense.'

'It was an act of God. But which God I'm not sure. There's so many of them. . But it doesn't matter you see because my task is complete.'

One of the office staff, came in, walking past their table.

'A pot of strong coffee and a couple of slices of wholemeal toast please, Marjorie. It's for Mr Solomons, so please put it on his account.'

Roddy turned to look at the woman and then back to Al.

'It's not possible, it's simply not possible.' He started to shake, muttering to himself.

Al went to his friend and helped him to his feet.

'Come on now, you need to lie down and then you and me are going to have a long chat.'

28

Saul stayed at the school on the Saturday night but couldn't persuade his brother to come out with him for a pub tea and a beer or two. The devastation of the fire had temporarily taken his mind off his meeting with John Bianchi, all he was expected to do at the bank and his commitment to stop gambling.

Despite the concern over their mother, what was troubling him most was the itch was back. He'd debated heading back to London and a session on the tables, but if he went to Rupert's then news of his appearance would quickly get back to the American. There were numerous other casinos he could go to, but something told him that crossing Bianchi was something you simply did not do. For now, he needed to focus on the problems here and the nagging doubt he had about his brother's involvement in the fire.

It was lunchtime the next day when they got the call that the forensic team had been given access to what remained of the house.

'Come on, let's get over there and see if there's any news. It's got to be better than hanging around here,' said Saul.

'You go if you want. I've got loads of stuff to do before Monday. Anyway, what are you expecting they'll find,' replied his brother.

'For Christ's sake, Bill. Our mother is missing. The odds are that she burned to death in her own home. We don't know how the fire started and you just sit there saying you're too bloody busy to get off your arse to go and find out what happened!'

'Look, Saul, I'm just being pragmatic. We can't change what they're going to find. As soon as they find out, they'll let us know. I don't see the point of hanging around all afternoon doing nothing when I can be getting on with preparing for the new term.'

His cold, unemotional tone cut through Saul like a knife through butter. He tried to find the right words to express his utter disbelief in what he was witnessing, but all he could manage was, 'Fine,' as he stormed out leaving his brother staring at the screen of his laptop.

It was a different policeman at the end of the drive, but he'd been given both brothers' names and allowed Saul to head up to the taped-off area, where he found DS Wilcox talking to the Fire Chief.

The policeman broke away from his conversation. 'Mr Solomons. I got your message yesterday, thanks.'

Saul nodded, but his eyes were drawn to the people in protective suits working amongst the remains of his family home. There was an eerie silence about the place, that he felt shouldn't be disturbed.

'Mr Solomons, Saul, we've found a body.'

He turned to the policeman.

'At the moment, all we can say is that it's the body of a female.'

'Can I see her?'

'Come and sit in my car.'

He led Saul to one of the police cars and sat him in the front passenger seat. He got behind the wheel and waited for a moment before continuing.

'The body was badly burned. We're going to need dental records to make the formal ID, but we are working on the assumption that it's Mrs Solomons. I'm very sorry for your loss Saul.' Another pause.

'Where's Bill? Would you like me to ring him?'

Saul almost laughed. 'He might not answer. He's preparing for the start of term. I doubt he'll have the time to pick up his phone.'

'Why do you think that is?'

Saul sighed, trying to hold back the tears that were slowly trickling down his cheeks.

'I don't know. Maybe it's the shock of it all. Bill and mother have been at odds recently. It wasn't the best way to leave things.'

'What do you mean?'

'We met with mother on Friday morning at the school. Solicitors were present. Bill and I were thinking of contesting our father's Will. It all feels so unseemly now that she's gone.'

'So, you didn't part on the best of terms?'

'I wouldn't say that. She was going to give us some of her own money, completely separate from what father left her. It wasn't as much as we needed. Bill got quite angry after she'd left.'

He was openly crying, but Wilcox sensed there was more to the story and it was important he got it now.

'What did you need the money for?'

Despite his emotions, Saul realised he'd said too much.

'Just our fair share. That's all. That's why it seems so stupid now. A lot of fuss over whose bank the money would sit in.'

The policeman continued, 'Look, it's important Bill knows that we've found a body. Why don't I drive you back to the school and we can tell him face to face?'

He didn't wait for Saul to answer. He started the car and drove slowly down the driveway, leaving the men and women of the forensic team to carry on their examination of what was increasingly looking like a murder site.

They found Bill in his office, talking on the phone to what sounded like a prospective parent, from his end of the conversation. Wilcox noted he made no attempt to end the call quickly, leaving the two of them shuffling around, staring at their shoes.

'Sorry about that. Just one of the parents of a new student wants to clarify a couple of things. Would you like some tea or coffee?'

Before the policeman could speak, Saul erupted, 'Do you have any idea why we're here! Why he might be here!' pointing at Wilcox. 'They've found a body at the house. It's almost certainly our mother and all you can do is worry about pacifying a prospective bloody parent!' He had his hands on his brother's desk and was yelling into his stunned face.

Wilcox intervened, pulling Saul away and getting him to sit in one of the chairs opposite his sibling. Shocked, Bill slumped back in his chair.

'I'm sorry Saul, I've been trying not to think about it. I thought if I buried myself in work this complete bloody mess would go away.'

Saul was slowly getting his breathing under control, but on a gesture from Wilcox didn't say anything, as the policeman tried to take the heat out of the situation.

'I suggest you both calm down. There's a great deal we need to discuss and whilst it's a very difficult time for you both, I suggest we do it now. OK?'

They both mumbled their agreement.

'First off, you'll both need to give formal statements. I suggest we do this at the station later today. This is routine in cases like this, so please don't read anything into it. I'll also need the details of your mother's dentist for identification purposes. It's important we identify the body as soon as possible. The forensic team will be on site for the rest of the day and probably tomorrow as well. They'll be able to tell us how the fire started and if any third party was involved.'

'Third-party?' said Saul. 'Do you think someone started the fire deliberately?'

'Again, this is routine, in a situation like this. All we are doing at the moment is establishing the facts. Once we've done that, we'll know what we're dealing with. Now, I need to ask you both about your mum, OK. Let's start with the details of her dentist.'

For the next hour, the brothers answered Wilcox's questions about their mother. Who her friends were, how often she saw them, what was her usual routine each day, the names of the housekeeper and the gardener and so on. Bill did most of the talking as Saul was clueless about any of the details of his mother's life.

'OK, that gives me a very comprehensive background. Now, I assume the house was insured?'

The question took Bill by surprise. 'Er, of course. I made sure it was renewed every year.'

'And the policy, is it in joint names?' asked Wilcox.

'Yes, it is. It was the sensible thing to do as we both lived there and meant I could deal with the renewal and any claims.'

'Of course, I understand,' said Wilcox.

With another change of topic, the policeman asked, 'When did your father die?'

Saul could see his brother was struggling with his emotions, so he stepped in. 'Last December. He had a heart attack on a business trip.'

There was a long pause while Wilcox made what must have been an extensive note in his little black book.

When he finished, he asked, 'So why are you contesting the will? Did something happen?'

Saul answered, 'Look, I know how it appears now that mother is dead, but it's not like that. When he was alive, father made it very clear to both of us that we were included in the Will. He was a very wealthy man and there was plenty to share around. His death was unexpected, so whether he hadn't got around to changing the details, no one knows, but everything and I mean everything was left to mother.'

Having composed himself Bill continued, 'We were surprised, shocked even. But most of all we were upset. It wasn't about the money; it was as though we didn't exist to him. No mention, no recognition, not even a small token to remember him by. We discussed it all with mother, but she was insistent that our father's wishes were followed to the letter. We couldn't let it go, but it rankles with us both.'

'So, back to my original question why get the solicitors involved?' asked Wilcox.

The brothers glanced at each other as if checking who would answer.

Saul got in first.

'It was a stupid idea. We were never going to see it through. We thought it might make mother see how pissed off we are. I mean, it's ludicrous. She's sitting on millions of pounds she'll never use and we've got all sorts of opportunities we could be pursuing.'

'What sort of opportunities?'

'Nothing specific, other than the freedom to live our lives without any financial constraints.'

Wilcox smiled. 'I understand and thanks for all the background. If you can come down to the station, we can get this on the record. OK?'

They nodded, following the policeman out of the room.

It took into the early evening for them to finish at the police station. They gave their statements separately, both repeating similar versions of what they'd told Wilcox earlier. They got dropped off at the house to pick up Saul's car, finally getting back at the school early evening.

It was another warm evening, so they sat on one of the benches in front of the main entrance.

'My head aches,' said Bill. 'Why did Wilcox get us to tell him everything and then have us repeat the same stuff all over again at the police station?'

'I'll tell you why,' replied his brother. 'Because he thinks one of us started the fire. I know it wasn't me Bill.'

He turned to look at his brother, his expression asking the question. Bill put his head in his hands and started to cry.

29

The table in the meeting room was surrounded with people. There was one free chair that Packham took, with two at the side of the room where Kell and Molly sat. A uniformed officer who Kell recognised as the Chief Superintendent, opened the meeting but didn't bother with introductions.

'Thanks to everyone for attending at short notice. I'd like to begin by asking DS Wilcox of the Hertfordshire Constabulary to brief us on a suspected murder that occurred over the weekend.'

'In the early hours of Saturday morning, a call was made to the emergency services in relation to a fire at a private residence in a secluded part of the countryside, ten miles from St Albans. The house is owned by Mrs Esther Solomons, who resided there with her eldest son, who is the headmaster at the nearby Wellington school. The forensic team's investigation is ongoing, however there is evidence that the fire was started deliberately. In the course of their investigation, the body of a woman was discovered. Earlier this morning, dental records confirmed that the body is that of Mrs Solomons.'

He paused as his flipped through his notebook.

'We have taken statements from William Solomons and his brother Saul, who was staying at the school for the weekend due to the bank he works for, being involved in the recent sale to new ownership. It is also worth mentioning that on Friday morning the brothers met with their mother at the school to discuss a potential contesting of the late husband's Will by them.'

Another pause. 'At the conclusion of the meeting on Friday, Mrs Solomons advised that she was leaving immediately, to go and stay at her house in Eastbourne. For a reason, we are yet to discover, she never went. At this point, we consider both of the Solomon brothers as suspects. I personally took their statements and both William and Saul provided "off the record" reasons why they believed their sibling was responsible for starting the fire.'

He nodded to no one in particular and sat down.

The Chief Super stood and much to Kell's surprise turned to him. 'Mr Kell, please can you update us on the murder of Emile Black.'

Trying not to show any nerves, Kell stood and gave a summary of how the missing person case had turned into a murder, concluding with how the body had been formally identified by Emile's partner Zornitsa Elianti.

'As part of our investigation, we interviewed Saul Solomons who has recently been appointed as the Head of anti-money laundering and financial crime prevention at Streem bank. It's our opinion that Saul Solomons was specifically targeted by the bank as Emile Black's replacement. We don't believe he was involved in the disappearance or subsequent murder, but he's certainly hiding something.'

On a nod from Packham, Kell sat down and he stood to address the room.

'Right, so we've got two murders, Emile Black and Esther Solomons, which on the face of it appear to be unrelated. Until that is you add in Streem Bank and the Solomon brothers. Streem has been under investigation by my cybercrime team for some time. We have intelligence that suggests they are a clearing house for the proceeds of crime. The investigation is ongoing and will continue for six to twelve months. Part of the investigation now includes the purchase of the Wellington private school, which we believe could be a front for washing through illegal cash.'

Packham sat down and one of the Security Services guys took his place. They were interested in the international aspect of the operation, overseas crime syndicates operating in the UK etc. And so, it went on, until virtually everyone in attendance had staked their claim of importance in the operation.

When it was clear that everyone had had their say, the Chief Super stood to bring the meeting to a conclusion.

'This is such a multi-dimensional investigation, that it would be ineffective and indeed impossible, to have a single chain of command. The two murder investigations will proceed independently. Chris's ongoing work with Streem will lead on the wider operation. This group will meet daily at 6.00 PM to share new information, particularly where operations may overlap. Any questions?'

A general shaking of heads and the briefing was over.

Packham walked over to Kell and Molly. 'Let's go to my office.'

Once they were settled around the small table, Molly went to speak, but Packham put up his hand to stop her. 'Let me go first, as there's some more work we'd like you to do.'

'We're all ears,' said Kell.

'It's to do with what Wilcox said about the Solomons' statements or should I say the "off the record" bit. Saul told the DS that his brother initially showed no interest in the seriousness of the fire and was uninterested in the whereabouts of their mother. Then when it was confirmed she died in the blaze, he went into the *Oh my god, what I have done* mode. He also states that it was Bill who was pushing for the money from the mother.'

Kell interrupted, 'Don't tell me, Bill says exactly the same thing about his brother.'

'On the money front yes. But he also said that Saul has a big gambling problem. Very big. Streem have given him advances on bonuses and salary to bail him out. All of which supports your theory that he was targeted by Bah and Canning.'

'Talking of which, what's happening down there at Streem?'

'A joint op from Essex and the Met. They are in there as we speak. The whole building has been designated a crime scene, but with a low profile. There isn't any yellow police tape across the front of the building. They're focusing on Canning as she's the last person who saw Emile alive, but all the senior people are under suspicion.'

'Make sure they speak to Emile's number two, his name's Pedro. He was the most forthcoming of all of them.'

'Noted.'

'So, what is it you want us to do?' asked Kell.

'Focus on Saul Solomons. Follow him. Track his every movement. Where he goes, who he sees. We'll provide you with live access to his personal and work mobiles, so you'll see who he's in contact with. And don't worry, it won't involve a lot of shoe leather. We can track his movements through his mobile. He's got a personal one and one for work. Molly, are you OK to continue with what you were doing the other day?'

'Actually, Chris, I wanted to talk to you about that. I'm really sorry, but I don't want to come and work here. I've given it a lot of thought and it's just not for me. I truly am sorry, but I've made my decision.'

'Oh,' was all Packham could manage.

Kell stood up. 'I think you should tell Chris everything we discussed. It's not been an easy decision and he deserves to know where you're coming from. I'll go and see if I can rustle up some drinks.'

Kell took his time finding the staff canteen and getting a couple of coffees and a peppermint tea for Molly. When he got to Packham's office, Molly smiled as he walked in.

'Everything OK?' he asked.

'Yes, everything's fine,' replied his friend. 'I don't think you planned it like this, but Molly's decision could mean we need to engage your services on a more formal retainer basis, whilst we finish the recruitment.'

'How so?'

'I think I can get approval for formally contracting with you, as in the business, for say twelve months, initially on the Streem work, but other cases as well. We'd contract for say half of Molly's time and one day a week for you. It'll help us bridge the staffing shortage and mean we won't lose too much traction with the investigations. This can all be done from Brick Lane, so you won't have to trek over here all the time. How does that sound?'

Molly smiled at her boss.

'Well, if you've convinced Molly, it's fine with me. Don't forget though, we've got some recruitment of our own to sort out.'

'Great, I'll sort the paperwork out and get a contract to you by the end of the week. Now, I need to crack on and you need to find Saul Solomons.'

*

Bill finally got his emotions under control and they sat for a few minutes without saying anything. Just as the older brother was about to speak one of the students came sprinting across the green towards them. Out of breath and clearly distressed, Al Stewart bent over with this hands on his knees, waiting to get his breath back. Eventually he managed.

'Mr Solomons, thank god you're OK. You've must come with me. It's Roddy. I think he tried to burn your house down.'

The brothers looked at each other, stunned, by what they'd heard.

'Come on, he's in the dorm. I think he's had a breakdown.'

Bill got up and started to follow the student who was sprinting towards the dorm block. Saul followed at a slow walk, thinking this might just provide the opportunity for both of them to come out of this scott free and not needing him to throw his brother under the proverbial bus.

30

Roddy got on his hands and knees and pulled the small metal box out from under his bed in the dormitory. He kept the key on a silver chain around his neck, which also held two crosses. One with Christ on the cross, one without.

He unlocked the box and pulled out a handful of the various pills and sachets of powder it contained. He was so tired he desperately needed a couple of uppers. He tipped the contents onto the floor and searched frantically for some speed that would keep him going for a bit longer. Anything that would give him a lift. When he was convinced he was out of luck, he lay on his back, trying to regulate his gasping breath. Since the end of term, he'd been relying more and more on the drugs to keep him going through the long days and nights of his religious research.

Then, eventually, he'd take something to get him to sleep and then start the cycle again. The problem he now had was his dealer had gone home for the summer and his stock had finally run out. He'd managed to hide his habit from his remaining friend and it was easier to do with hardly anyone around. But he knew that Al suspected something, especially when he started experimenting with mushrooms and sometimes couldn't remember where he'd been or what he'd done. Anyway, maybe it was time to give the drugs a break and head home for the last couple of weeks of the summer break.

He gathered up the mess he strewn over the floor, put it back in the box, locked it and pushed it under his bed. His body was telling him it needed to sleep, so he curled up on his bed and was drifting into the land of dreams when Al burst into the room.

'Roddy, are you OK?'

Pushing himself up onto one elbow, he slowly came to and took in the scene in front of him.

'What's he doing here?'

'I'm worried about you mate. You were acting all weird, talking to yourself, like you were in a trance. I went to get Mr Solomons because I think you need help.'

'Help, from him! You've got to be joking. All I need is some sleep. I've been working very hard recently.'

Al sat on the bed and put his arms around his friend's shoulders. 'We just want to help you, Rod. You've been acting very strange the last few weeks and by that, I mean more strange than normal.'

Roddy laughed. 'I'm just different from you. Occasionally, I might take something to help me see the world from a different perspective, but I can assure you I'm not going mad. Now, if you'll excuse me, I need to get some sleep.'

'Rod, we need to talk to you about the other night. You know, the fire. You were there weren't you?'

The vacant look that Al had gotten so used to seeing in his friend's eyes, spread across his face. 'Ah yes, the fire. I made all that effort. All those plans for nothing.'

Bill stepped forward. 'What do you mean, it was all for nothing? My mother died in that fire.'

Saul came into the room and took in the scene. Roddy stared at him, then back at the headmaster.

'Are you two brothers? You do look alike,' he asked.

'Yes, this is my brother Saul. Now why did you set my house on fire, you little shit?'

Roddy sat on the bed shaking his head. 'No, no, no. You've got that all wrong Mr Solomons, it wasn't me that started the fire, but I saw who did.' He turned and looked at Saul. 'Don't I, the other Mr Solomons.'

Al interjected. 'What do you mean, Rod? You had all sorts of stuff in your rucksack when you staggered in the other morning. I had a look. Old fireworks, matches, a bottle of turpentine. You went to the house to set it on fire.'

'Oh Al, you never were the sharpest tool in the box. If I went to start the fire, why would all those essential ingredients you listed still be in my rucksack? Wouldn't I have used them to start the conflagration? Look, the truth is by the time I got there, it's such a long way to walk, by the way, the house was already ablaze and I assumed our tiresome headmaster was meeting his maker, like the heretics in 16th century. His car was there you see.'

Bill was trying very hard not to thump the smart-arsed little prick. He took a deep breath.

'We need to let the police handle this. Come on, I'll take you to the station and let's see what they make of this fairy tale you've concocted. Saul, you're coming too.'

But his brother was not there. He slipped out and was on his way back to London.

'Looks like he's got something better to do, which, as it happens, so do I. I really need to get some sleep, so if you'll excuse me, I'll say goodnight.'

Roddy rolled over onto his side and was asleep the second his head hit the pillow.

'What are we going to do now?' asked Al.

Bill was already walking out of the dorm, shaking his head. 'I'm going to make a couple of phone calls. One to the police, who need to handle this. They'll want to speak to you as well, but I guess it can wait till the morning. Solomons walked to his office leaving Al, wondering what was going to happen next.

His first call was to Wilcox. It went straight to voicemail, so he asked him to give him a call when convenient. No rush, nothing urgent.

Then he rang his brother. 'Where the bloody hell are you? Why did you disappear like that?'

'I'm in the car heading back to London. I got a text from Abebe, I'm needed back in the office first thing in the morning. Anyway, the kid is clearly delusional. Him and his mate are just attention seekers, trying to make mischief in the boring summer holiday.'

Bill let out an exhausted sigh. 'You're probably right. I've left a message for Wilcox. He can speak to him, see if he can make any sense of his nonsense. Look, I'm sorry for yelling at you, it's just with the fire, mother's death, the school, idiot students, it's all getting too much. I don't know how much more I can take.'

'Hey, I know what it's like to feel like that. All the shit I've been involved with over the years. Get a good night's sleep and it won't seem quite so bad in the morning. Let's take one step at a time. I'll come back up next weekend, OK. In the meantime, keep me posted with any developments.'

Saul ended the call, satisfied his brother hadn't clocked the look that the one called Roddy had given him. It was yet another bump in the road that needed sorting but for now, he had only one thing on his mind. He'd lied about getting a text from his boss, but not about the urgency of getting back to London. He needed to gamble. To play roulette. To satisfy what was now an unbearable itch. To hell with Bianchi and his macho posturing, he planned to have a big night, a very big night.

He knew it would be stupid to go to Rupert's, so he decided to stick close to home. He'd been to the casino in the Canary Wharf shopping centre a couple of times. It wasn't his favourite spot, but it was only a 15-minute taxi ride from where he lived and it had some higher-stakes tables. He'd convinced himself that the likelihood of Bianchi finding out he'd been there was remote.

Anyway, he was an important member of the team at the bank. They needed him and he doubted they could survive the disappearance of another Compliance and Financial Crime expert. He checked the sat nav. One hour and four minutes until he was home. He'd be at the table in less than an hour and a half.

He knew the Wharf Casino wasn't in the same chain as Rupert's, which reduced the already slim chance that the American would hear of his night out. He signed in as a guest for the evening and made his way to the quietest table he could find. Being Sunday night, the place was quiet. The main business days here were mid-week when the thousands of office workers sought the opiate of gambling.

On the drive down, he'd been thinking about his various systems and whether he should stick to one of them or simply play freestyle. There are 18 red and 18 black numbers on the wheel. Most punters think this gives them a 50/50 chance of an even money payout if you choose correctly. What most punters don't realise, is the significance of the green 0. This means that over a long period, (he'd never considered how long this actually was) consistently playing either red or black would lose you money.

The rewards of such a system were also poor. You only doubled your money on one spin, to often lose it on the next when the other colour got spun in. Quite simply, to win big, you needed to bet on single numbers, which paid out at 35/1. It was a higher risk strategy, but now he had plenty of funds, it was the one he decided he'd run with tonight. Ten numbers, £50 a number. A successful spin returns £1800 including the stake. A profit of £1300. A good place to start. He sat at the table and started playing.

After ten spins, he hadn't had a win. He was down £5,000, so he did what most players did if they could afford it he doubled up.

There were times during his five hour stay that he nearly got back to even. On the last occasion, he saw this as a sign that his luck had changed and increased his stakes again. He left with the first light of dawn starting to shimmer on the Thames, with a bank balance that was significantly reduced but on the bright side, still in credit.

31

It was Monday evening. Bah, Hall, Canning and Bianchi sat in a private room in a gentleman's club in Mayfair that Bah and Hall were members of.

Bah opened the impromptu board meeting. 'Right, Suzie, you'd better share with us how your marathon interrogation by the police went.'

'It certainly was a very long day. To begin with, they spent ages trying to dig into my past. They asked questions about what I did at university, who my friends were, are they still my friends and so on. Then it was a forensic examination of my work life, all the jobs I've had, who I worked for, who worked for me. Names, dates, places. I'd forgotten half of the stuff until they started asking questions about it.

Then there was a lot about how I was recruited at Streem, did I know anyone in the bank before I joined, the working relationships with everyone. All in all an incredible amount of detail. That took all morning before we had a twenty-minute break for lunch. After that, it was all about Emile Black. Again, how he was recruited, who his friends were, working relationships. All the same stuff they asked me. Next, the focus was on his personnel file, particularly the warnings he'd had.'

Bah interrupted, 'Did they bring this up or did you offer it?'

'They brought it up. They'd clearly been through his file in detail and they also had the details of what that Kell guy had asked me.'

'How much did they question about our concerns that Black's work had deteriorated and that he may be helping certain outside organisations?'

'Not so much at first. It was as though they either didn't believe it or thought it wasn't relevant. It was only when we got on to the day he came in to hand his notice in, that their interest piqued.'

She paused for a sip of her gin and tonic.

'Throughout the interview, I stressed that Emile and I were on good terms, despite having to issue him with a verbal and written warning. I explained that when he confirmed his decision he was resigning, he got emotional and started crying.

At first, he said, he was just doing a favour for these businesses in exchange for cash and gifts, but once it became a regular thing and he wanted out, they started threatening him and his girlfriend. It was when he told them he was resigning, that they threatened to kill him. He thought he'd been followed on his way to the bank and asked if he could leave through the service entrance in the basement. He'd get a friend to pick him up from the service road at the back.'

'Do you think they believed you?' asked Bianchi.

'I don't know. But there's no evidence to the contrary.'

'But you didn't tell the investigator, Kell, this did you?' asked Bah.

'No, I didn't. But he's only a PI, not the police and I wasn't sure what side he was on. Anyway, there's no evidence of any foul play taking place within the bank.'

There were nods and murmurs of good job, well done from the others.

'The only potential loose end is Pedro Sanchez, Emile's number two. He emailed in his resignation over the weekend, saying he was very stressed by the death of his boss and he was going back to Barcelona. He asked if we'd pay his full three months' notice.'

'I see. I'll get one of our Spanish contacts to keep an eye on Sanchez. We need to be certain there are no weak links.'

Having listened intently to the conversation, Bianchi spoke for the first time.

'Saul Solomons is a weak link. You need to do something about him.'

They looked at him waiting for the American to continue.

'You know he has a gambling problem. I introduced myself at the Rupert's casino last week, preventing him from losing even more than the thousands he'd already lost. I wrote off his debt and had a long chat with him over dinner, making it clear that if he didn't stop, he'd be out of a job or worse. He's very concerned about the two mill, him and his brother have to find for the school. He asked me if I'd lend it to them and of course, I said no. He told me he had plans of his own as to how he could get it and the next thing his ma's house burns down with her inside it.'

'Are you suggesting he started the fire,' said an incredulous Bah.

'I'm hearing that the police have evidence that it was started deliberately. So if it wasn't one of the brothers then who was it? They have an awful lot to gain from their mother's death.'

'What do you propose we do?' asked Hall.

'Before I answer that, there are a couple of other problems.'

'Go on.'

'Yesterday, he spent most of the night at the casino in Canary Wharf, losing tens of thousands of pounds. The guy isn't stable.'

'You said there were two problems,' said Bah.

'Yeh, he disobeyed an order and that's not allowed.' The room went quiet as they took in what he'd said.

When he thought they'd fully digested the implications, he continued, 'Guys like Saul are ten a penny. There are hundreds of them out there, you just need to find the right one. As I understand it, he doesn't formally start working for you until 1 September, so I propose you withdraw the offer.'

Hall looked worried. 'But what if he goes to the police? He knows all about the school and he's also started to make certain of the regulatory checks appear OK.'

'Simple, you threaten you'll kill him if he breathes a word to anyone. You can't permanently silence him now, so you pay him to disappear overseas. With his gambling problem, it's an easy sell. He'll bite your hand off.'

Another silence ensued until Bah gave his verdict.

'Very well, I agree. Unless anyone has any issues with what John proposes, I suggest that we call him in and Suzie makes sure it's done by the book from an HR perspective. Offer him six months salary and the usual NDA. John, you will need to spell out the consequences of what will happen to him if he says anything that he shouldn't. As soon as the matter of the fire is over, he should leave the country.'

'I can take over the necessary regulatory checks until we find a replacement, but we're very thin on the ground with Pedro Sanchez leaving as well. I recommend we advertise through the usual agencies for experienced contract staff, alongside the permanent recruitment piece.'

'Agreed, Francis. We'll meet at close of play tomorrow to see where we are up to.'

As they packed up their papers, Bianchi said to Canning, 'How do you want to handle the meeting with Saul? Do you want me there or shall I see him when you've finished your bit?'

'For effect, I think we should see him together. Once I've advised him, we are withdrawing the offer and he's signed the NDA, I'll leave you to it. How does that sound?'

'Perfect, can you get him in first thing, I've got a busy day tomorrow with other clients.'

'Of course, 9 o'clock, OK?

Bianchi nodded. 'See you then.'

Saul wasn't surprised to get the summons from the HR director that he was needed for an important meeting in the morning. But he was very surprised when he sauntered in at 9.00 AM to see John Bianchi sitting next to her.

'Thanks for coming in, Saul, please take a seat. I'll get straight to the point. The board have decided to withdraw the offer of employment. You will not be starting on 1st September. As a sign of goodwill for the help you've provided in the last few weeks, we will pay you for six months. This is on the conditions stated in this Non-Disclosure Agreement, which you will sign now.'

She smiled as she pushed the papers across the table to him.

'But, what about—'

'The matter is not for debate, please sign the forms Saul and then Mr Bianchi wants a word.' Saul flipped through the three pages of A4. 'What do they say?'

It was Bianchi who answered. 'Words to the effect that if you breathe a word about what you've been involved with recently, one of my men will find you and gut you. So sign and then you and me are going for a walk.'

32

Kell and Molly had been at work since 7.30 AM, wanting to make sure they didn't miss any of Saul Solomons' whereabouts. Staring intently at her laptop screen, Molly saw the first movements as the flashing dot indicated he'd left home and was heading for the DLR.

'He's on the move, heading towards the station. Does it track him when he's on the underground?'

'According to Chris, yes it does. Anyway, we're about to find out. I guess he's either heading into his current employer to tidy things up before he leaves or more likely he's on his way to Streem. They must be getting very twitchy with everything that's going on.'

At 8.45 AM, the dot moved away from the tube station at St Pauls. 'He's definitely heading to Streem,' said Molly.

'Right, I'm heading over there. Hopefully, I can see who he's with when he comes out.'

'But he could be in there all day! It's a long time to hang around trying to look inconspicuous,' said Molly.

'Not all PI work is glamourous, you know. I've done my fair share of stakeouts and observation duties and believe me, they're incredibly boring. Anyway, this will be easier as you can ring me when he starts moving.'

Kell was in a coffee shop on the opposite side of the road, fifty yards south of the entrance to the bank. The place was quiet and he settled into a window seat, got his laptop out and ordered a large Americano. As soon as his drink arrived his mobile rang.

'Doesn't look like you'll have a long wait darling. He's on the move and should be appearing at any moment.'

'Not a long meeting then. Good job I got my coffee to go. Stay on the line so I can keep you updated.'

A minute later Saul appeared with another man who although Kell had never met, he recognised from the various pictures he'd seen.

'Well, that is interesting. Our Mr Solomons has just come out of the bank with none other than the mysterious John Bianchi.'

'What do you want me to do? Shall I let Chris know?' asked Molly.

'No, let me see where they're heading. The police haven't got anything on Bianchi, so I'm not sure they've got any reason to pick him up. That doesn't stop me from having a quiet word though.'

'Be careful, Justin. Remember, Chris said just to follow him and see who he meets.'

'There's nothing to be worried about. I'm hanging up. I'll give you a call later.'

Molly put the phone down and felt another anxious twinge in her stomach. She was beginning to understand how his previous girlfriend, Amy, felt when she said he charged into situations without thinking. It had finally driven them apart and she was beginning to worry if the same thing could be happening again.

Coffee in hand, Kell followed Saul and Bianchi from the opposite side of Farringdon Street. They were heading towards the river and it was Bianchi who appeared to be doing all the talking. As they approached Blackfriars, Bianchi led Saul into a small park where they sat side by side on one of the benches.

'Did you really think I wouldn't find out about your trip to the Canary Wharf casino?'

Saul sat there shaking his head and not replying.

'Not only that but you lost big again! What sort of gambler are you? Now, I suggest you go home, pack a bag and get on the first flight out of here. Or get on a train and head to France.' Saul finally managed, 'But where would I go?'

'I'd head to Africa but suggest you break up the journey. Do some hitchhiking, make yourself inconspicuous. You're never going to work in financial services again and you'll go to prison if they catch you, so the sooner you leave the better. And remember what I said. Not one word.'

Kell watched them for five minutes, noting it was still the American doing all the talking with Saul looking more nervous by the minute. When Saul stood up to leave and Bianchi pulled him back down to the bench, he decided it was time to step in. He approached them from behind, so when he asked if he could join them, they both turned around in surprise.

Kell stood in front of the two seated men. 'Let me introduce myself, Mr Bianchi. I'm Justin Kell and we must have just missed each other, up in Manchester last year. Saul, we've already met.'

Calm and assured as ever, Bianchi stood and shook hands with Kell.

'Pleased to meet you Justin, but I don't recall being in, where did you say, last year?'

'Manchester, but that's not important. It's Saul I'm here to speak to, but you're very welcome to stay.'

'Actually, I'm done here. I've got another appointment I need to get to. Nice to meet you, Justin. And Saul, remember what I said.' He turned and walked out of the small park.

Opposite the park entrance, two black cabs stood at a small rank. Bianchi spoke to the driver of the front taxi but then got in the back of the second and waited.

Kell watched Bianchi until he left the park, before sitting down next to Saul.

'Didn't look like the friendliest of chats. You need to be very careful around John Bianchi, he's a very dangerous man.'

'Tell me about it. How on earth did I end up in all this. I've just been sacked from a job that I haven't officially started and I've got the mafia threatening to kill me if I breathe a word about anything!'

'Ah, so that was why you were just at the bank. Who did you see?'

'Suzie. It was brutal. You're not joining us, the offer is withdrawn, sign this NDA. And then I get the hard word from Bianchi saying that if say anything to anyone, I'm a dead man. In fact, speaking to you now, I've probably signed my own death warrant.'

'Let's get a couple of things straight. What crimes have you actually committed and more importantly what crimes are you aware of that Bah and his cronies are responsible for?'

'How long have you got,' said Saul. 'I've knowingly facilitated money laundering. Not undertaken certain checks, falsified the findings of checks that we didn't like. Falsified documents. Put it this way it's enough to put me away for ten years. Oh and I'm a terrible roulette player as well if that counts as a crime.'

'And what about the guys at Streem?' asked Kell.

'It's a very sophisticated operation. They've got numerous dodgy clients, who continually push dirty money through the bank. They wash it through and it comes back clean. They're about to start using our friend Bianchi. He's got a cryptocurrency that speeds up the washing of the cash. I'm not sure if they've agreed on terms yet, but they must be close. The whole place stinks of corruption.'

'What about the fire at the house? Did you start it?' Kell decided that being blunt was best.

'No, it wasn't me. I thought it must be Bill, but I really don't see him doing something like that. It was just the way he acted when we heard mother had died. Well, it got me thinking. Then there's this weird student who says he was at the fire. I don't know what to make of it all.'

'Look, we've got to get you to a police station. I'm sure there's a deal to be done if you testify against the Bah and Canning. Come on, let's get moving before he comes back with his heavies.'

They hurried out of the park, crossed the road and jumped in the taxi at the head of the rank.

Bianchi smiled as he watched them get in the cab in front of him. He spoke into his phone. 'They're on their way. Less than five minutes. I've got a meeting with a potential client, but I'll check in later. My clean-up team should be there by midday.'

He ended the call.

'The City Hotel Fenchurch Street. Then if you wait five minutes while I check out, I'm heading to Heathrow. I'll make it worth your while.'

He was a smart guy. He knew when to get out of Dodge. Things were going badly wrong and he wasn't going to stick around and get caught up in the shitstorm.

'Bishopsgate police station, please,' said Kell.

The taxi pulled away heading north up Farringdon Street. Kell wasn't paying any particular attention to where the taxi was heading, but when it turned across the traffic into a side road and the then quickly left into a small service road, he instinctively tried the door of the black cab, which was locked, of course. He shouted to the driver to stop and let them out.

When that didn't work, he banged on the Perspex screen desperately trying to get his attention. The taxi then turned down a ramp into a service area which he immediately recognised. He'd been here before.

Saul Solomons had started sobbing beside him. He heard him mutter, 'Please god, no.'

The taxi stopped in front of the plant room. The driver got out and walked over to the kiosk were the attendant stepped out to speak to him. Kell watched a brief conversation before the attendant walked up the ramp and pressed the large red button, that brought the steel shutters down. He retrieved his jacket from the back of his chair and walked over to the lift, that Kell had used on his previous visit. The taxi driver remained by the bottom of the ramp, making a call on his mobile.

Kell tried the door again, but to no avail. He then sat back in his seat and tried kicking at the Perspex screen that separated them from the front of the cab. He felt it start to give but was distracted by a tap on the window. The taxi driver was standing next to his door pointing a gun at them. Suzie Canning stood next to him, smiling.

'Hello again, Mr Kell.' She had to raise her voice to a near shout to make herself heard. 'Please try and be patient. Mr Bianchi's colleagues will be here shortly and we'll let you out. then. Now open the window and pass me your phones. And please don't try and be the hero.' Dimitri here has a very itchy finger. They passed their phones to Canning, who tossed them onto the floor. 'Thank you, now close the window.'

She looked at Saul and simply shook her head, before, turning around and getting into the service lift.

*

Bianchi walked up to the first-class check-in desk for his flight to New York. He handed over his passport to the smiling attendant who ran through the standard questions. He got the sense that something was wrong when she stepped away from the counter and he turned around to be confronted by a man in plain clothes, accompanied by two armed police officers.

'If you could come with us please, Mr Bianchi. We need to ask you a few questions.'

33

For Roderick Roan, the concept of "normality" was something he'd never considered. Some of his earliest memories included being referred to as "not normal". Culprits included his father and the nanny who looked after him in his pre-school years. They didn't say this to his face, but he overheard conversations with his mum, who was the only person who seemed to understand him.

There was one moment that stood out above all others. It was the day of his eighth birthday and he would be changing schools after the summer holidays. His dad was adamant that he would go to the same prep school that he'd attended all those years ago and which would mean he had to board full-time.

His mum wanted to send him locally, pleading with her husband that eight was far too young to send a child away from home, no matter how good the school was. He sat at the top of the stairs listening as the argument got louder and louder until finally his mother burst into tears and ran out of the house slamming the door behind her.

He felt guilty that it was his fault his adoring mum had apparently left him. All he could remember of his dad's ranting was how he kept saying that their only child wasn't normal. He wasn't normal and his mum had left because of him.

Of course, she hadn't left. He found out the next morning, again from his vantage point at the top of the stairs, that she'd walked around the gardens that surrounded the house until she managed to stop crying. He was so relieved that she hadn't left because of him, but then the hammer blew. She agreed with his dad that he would be sent away to school.

She'd had time to think it over and he was right. It would do Roddy good. Give him the chance to focus on his learning. Become independent. Make new friends.

He remembered how horrible he felt that summer. Terrified at the thought of being sent away because now, even his mum didn't love him enough to want him to live at home with her. For the seven weeks of that long summer holiday, he barely spoke to anyone, spending his time roaming in the nearby woods, playing imaginary games, making imaginary friends and having make-believe conversations with them.

On the day they drove him to what he thought of as the other side of the world but was in fact just eighty miles towards the coast, he didn't say a word. When they all got out of the car and were met by the headteacher and two of the older pupils who took his bags to the dormitory, he couldn't look at either of his parents. He clumsily hugged his mum around her waist, not wanting to let go, but when he was pulled away, he didn't say goodbye.

He remembered his mum crying, which made him think that maybe she did love him, but his father stood, stern-faced as he was led away into the hell that was the next three years of his life.

Kids can be cruel. Very cruel. The bullying and pranks were worse in the first term. His bed was urinated on. His clothes went missing along with his schoolbooks and at first, when he went to his House Master, he'd end up in a fight with at least two of his so-called classmates.

He made one friend that term, Warwick Husker. For some reason, he missed the focus of the bullying and was the only person who tried to stop the antics and comforted him when he was left crying on his bed.

When they returned after the Christmas holiday, things started to slowly get better. The practical jokes stopped, along with the bullying. There was still the occasional confrontation but as he finally settled into the rhythm of boarding school life, Roddy began to feel that this strange place that he'd hated for the last six months was starting to feel like home.

His friendship with Warwick became brotherly. And when the summer term ended, they shared their time at each other's homes. They simply did everything together. Studied, played sport, enjoyed riding their ponies and playing in the fields and woods like all children did.

Academically, they were matched. Their grades in each subject mirrored the others and when the time finally came for them to move schools, there was no doubt in their minds that they'd be going together.

Of course, their parents, specifically their fathers did not share the same view. Warwick came from a large family of three brothers and a sister. They had all attended Harrow and that was where Warwick would be going. Roddy could tell his dad didn't like Warwick.

Whenever he visited, he ignored him. His mum was pleasant enough, but he could sense there was something she didn't like about his only friend. Whether it was for this reason they decided Roddy should go to the less renowned Wellington School in Hertfordshire or simply that it was a cheaper option, he never found out.

Surprisingly, there was only one major scene, when his dad told him the decision was final. He remembered many bad things being said by him and his dad. He was a child, but he meant it when he said he hated his father and would never forgive him for what he'd done. From that day to this, they hadn't spoken. Whenever he needed anything, he'd ring or text his mum.

And here he was at Wellington. He surprised himself at how quickly he forgot about Warwick. He quickly made friends with his three dormers, settled into his studies and started to feel just that bit happier with his lot.

But he often questioned what happiness was. His friends talked fondly about their families and life at home and he got embarrassed when they asked about his mum and dad and family holidays. He was non-committal, vague in his replies. He even thought about pretending that Warwick was his brother, but realised he'd already told them he was an only child.

Then the problems with Dr William Solomons started. He reminded him so much of his father, that from that first English Literature lesson, he hated him. His friends had gone along with making Doc Solomons the epitome of all that was bad at Wellington, but he knew there were times that they simply humoured him.

Over the years, the tension between him and the teacher had intensified and as he lay on his bed in their dorm, waiting for the police to come and take him away for questioning, he thought the symmetry of the setting fire to the curtains in the Main Hall and what had happened at Solomons home. It was somewhat ironic. One fire he definitely started and one he wasn't quite sure what had happened.

He was torn away from his early morning daydream when the door opened and Solomons and another man walked in, with Al trailing behind them.

'Good morning, Roddy, I'm DS Wilcox and I'd like you to come to the police station with me so I can ask you a few questions about the fire at Mr Solomons's house.'

Roddy almost jumped up off his bed, giving the DS his broadest smile. 'Of course, officer. I'd be delighted to come with you. Will I be able to have some breakfast? I'm absolutely ravenous!'

Wilcox nodded, not replying and led Roddy down to one of the waiting police cars.

Al and Solomons watched him go, before getting into the second car. They all had lots of questions to answer.

As soon as they arrived at the station, Wilcox showed Roddy to the staff canteen and told him to get what he wanted, 'At this stage, you're simply helping us with our enquiries. And you're free to leave at any time you like. Would you like me to contact your parents? They can sit on the interview if you prefer or I can arrange for one of our FLOs to attend if you prefer.'

Roddy was aghast at the thought of seeing his father and started shaking his head. 'No, no, no, no. I don't want to see my dad. My mum's OK, but not my dad.'

'Shall I call your mum then?'

More shaking of the head. 'No, no, not my mum either.'

Wilcox shrugged. 'OK, that's fine. I'll be back in twenty minutes. I'll leave you with PC McKay. He'll make you sure you get what you want.'

Roddy suddenly found he'd lost his appetite as the gravity of the situation started to hit home. He picked at some toast and managed half a mug of lukewarm tea. What if he had started the fire? What if he was responsible for the death of Solomon's mum. Would his parents think they were right all along and he wasn't normal? All these thoughts were spinning in his head as he stared into his empty mug, waiting for the DS to reappear.

Once they were settled in the interview room, Wilcox repeated that Roddy was there to provide a statement on the events surrounding the fire at the Solomon house and he was free to leave at any time he wanted. He introduced the Family Liaison Officer, who was sitting at the back of the room and was there because he was only seventeen.

The questions started with Wilcox asking about his time at the school. What subjects he did, who his friends were, how did he like boarding and what he planned to do when he finished at Wellington in twelve months' time. He answered easily and confidently, until the question about his future.

'I suppose that depends if you lock me up for starting the fire.'

Slightly taken aback by the response Wilcox asked, 'Did you start the fire, Roddy?'

Roddy thought hard, trying to recollect the evening in question. 'You see the thing is, I'm not sure. I know I went to the house, but it wasn't to set fire to it. When I got there, it was already ablaze. It was beautiful. I was in awe at the glory of it.'

'Why did you walk all that way to the house, Roddy?'

'I had an idea about a prank I could play on the Doc. I had some old fireworks and was going to set them off to frighten him and wake him up. But someone had already started the bonfire by the time I got there.'

'But why did you want to prank Mr Solomons in the first place?'

'Oh, that's easy. I don't like him and he doesn't like me.'

'I see. Is there anything else you can tell me about that night. Anything at all?'

There was a pause before he answered as if he was trying to remember the scene.

Eventually, he said, 'Yes. He was there as well.'

'Who was there, Roddy?'

'Why Mr Solomons, of course. Or it could have been his brother. They look very alike don't you think.'

'Let me get this straight. You're saying that you saw Mr Solomons or possibly his brother at the house when it was on fire?'

'Yes, absolutely 100%. I'll swear on all the Bibles I've read.'

'OK, that's all for the time being, Roddy. Would you mind waiting in the canteen while I consider what you've told us.'

The same PC led him down to the canteen and feeling much better, his appetite returned. He was looking forward to a late breakfast.

Wilcox looked at the FLO, who was still making notes at the back of the room.

'What did you make of that?' he asked.

'I think he's a very disturbed young man and I strongly recommend getting our medical team to speak to him. As to whether he started the fire, I've absolutely no idea. Although it's a stretch, he was capable of doing so.'

'I agree. Can I leave you to get the doc down here pronto and sit with him when he speaks to Roddy? I think it's time I put some serious questions to Bill Solomons. There's something about him and his story that just doesn't add up.'

Al's statement hadn't taken long to get down on paper. He simply repeated all he could recall about the night in question and run through the background of his friendship with Roddy. He smiled when his friend walked in and after a clumsy hug, they sat at the table in the far corner of the room.

'How did it go?' asked Al.

Roddy started nodding his head with a look of consternation on his face. 'How did it go? Now that's an interesting question. Not like the questions the policeman asked me, which were normal questions. It's easy to answer to normal questions if you know the answer that is.'

Al wasn't surprised by the opaqueness of his friend's response, so he got straight to the point. 'Did you start the fire at Doc Solomons's house?'

Roddy looked up, his eyes clear and focussed as he looked at Al. 'No, I didn't, but I think it was Mr Solomons who did.'

*

Bill looked at his watch for the umpteenth time. He was asked to wait in a rather bleak interview room over an hour ago and hadn't even had the offer of a cup of tea! He tried opening the door to go and find someone who could tell him what was going on, but unsurprisingly it was locked. With nothing to do, he sat down and waited.

When Wilcox finally appeared, accompanied by a fresh-faced PC, he was about to kick off. That was until he saw the look on the Detective Sergeant's face.

34

Molly watched the red dot on her screen move north up Farringdon Street. This told her that Saul was on the move but was Justin with him? She watched as the dot zig-zagged on the screen and came to stop. She moved the zoom up and down until she could see exactly where what she assumed was a car or taxi had stopped. She froze when she saw it either right outside or in the underground service area at Streem. She grabbed her phone and speed-dialled Kell. It rang five times before diverting to voicemail. In the taxi, Kell heard the ring and prayed that Molly would know what to do next.

She did. She immediately rang Packham who incredibly answered on the first ring. Molly knew she had to stay calm and considered so as soon as Packham asked what he could do for her.

She began, 'Earlier this morning, Justin was watching the bank for Saul Solomons. He came out of the bank at approximately 9.30 with John Bianchi and he followed them down Farringdon Street. The next thing, Saul is moving back up Farringdon quickly, most likely in a cab. The tracking device shows he's probably in the underground area below Streem. I've tried ringing Justin, but it goes to voicemail. I think they're both in trouble, Chris. Please can you get down there as fast as you can.'

'Bloody typical! Leave it with me, Mol, I'll have an armed unit down there in twenty minutes. In the meantime, you stay put and ring me if you hear from him.' He ended the call and Molly got that sickly feeling in her stomach and ran to the bathroom.

Molly stared at the phone and her mind went blank. She felt numb and was terrified at what might be happening to the love of her life. Next thing, she was walking down a rundown street with Jimmy Skaa pushing her along, hurrying her towards a place she didn't want to go to. She didn't want to go into the house, she knew that if she did then she wouldn't come out alive, would never see Justin again, would never see anyone again other than the crazed maniac that was Skaa.

Her subconscious told her that what she was experiencing wasn't real, it was her mind flashing back to the same recurring nightmare, although this time it was replaying the whole episode from start to finish. She could picture the cellar, the chains on the walls and the floor, the man who was already in there with her. What was name? She knew it but couldn't quite bring it to the forefront of her mind. Did it matter what his name was? Of course not he would soon be killed in horrific circumstances by Skaa. Would he kill her as well? Of course not. She's alive and this is just a dream. Isn't it?

Then the scene changes and she's holding a gun. Is the gun loaded? Why would the madman give her a gun? Why doesn't she shoot him and have done with it? But the gun isn't loaded of course, he wants her to hold it to her head so he can take a photograph of her. Why does he want to take a photograph? Then she remembers, he's going to send it to Justin and then he'll come and save her. But that's not right, is it?

The madman wants to hurt Justin, in fact it's more than that he wants to kill him. Dread fills her as she realises she's going to watch her lover die at the hands of a lunatic. She needs to warn him not to come, that it's a trap, but she's chained up and she can't reach her phone. But where is her phone?

And then another shock of realisation when he's using it to send Justin the picture. If only she had a phone and then slowly she realises she does. It's in her hand. Relief floods through her as she understands she's in the office on Brick Lane and she's safe. But as she returns from the flashback, the first thing that hits her is that this time it's Justin that's in danger and there's nothing she can do to help him.

Kell didn't take his eyes off the man with the gun, desperately trying to figure out a plan for when they were let out of the cab. Anyone hired by Bianchi would be ruthless, so whatever opportunity presented itself, they'd have to move fast.

'Now Saul, listen very carefully and for Christ's sake pull yourself together. When they let us out of here, get yourself as far away from me as you can. I'll do all the talking and try and cause a scene. As soon as you get the chance run and pray that they leave the shutters open.'

The timing was apt as Saul's reply was interrupted by the sound of the shutters slowly being raised.

A white transit van drove slowly down the ramp. It carefully did a three-point turn and reversed up to the side of cab nearest to where Saul was sitting. Solomons was a wreck.

He'd managed to curl up into the foetal position and was lying on the floor of the taxi. Whatever Kell was going to do, he'd have to do on his own.

Three men got out of the front of the van. One went to the kiosk and the shutters started to descend. Once they were shut, he pulled a gun and stood facing the taxi. The other two had a brief conversation with the man standing guard before they moved to either side of the cab by the rear doors. The third man opened the driver's door and released the central locking system.

'Mr Kell, Mr Solomons, please open your doors and slowly get out of the vehicle.'

Kell knew he had to delay the inevitable as long as he could. 'Unfortunately, Mr Solomons isn't very well. He's had some sort of panic attack; it looks like he's out cold on the floor.'

Kell could hear Saul's whimpering but doubted the men outside could. 'Listen, Saul, if you want to get out of this alive, stop crying like a baby. Just lie there and pretend to be unconscious.'

He didn't reply, but Kell was relieved when the crying stopped.

The two men outside had a brief conversation in a language Kell didn't recognise, before reverting to English with the next instruction.

'Very well. That makes it easier for us. Mr Kell, please step out of the vehicle, with your hands in the air. Any sudden movement and I will shoot you.'

'But what about Saul, I think he needs an ambulance!'

The man holding the gun laughed loudly. 'I don't think so, Mr Kell. Ambulances are for the living. Now please, I ask for the last time. Get out of the car.'

Packham walked down to the Chief Super's office shouting instructions into his mobile. He didn't bother knocking and quickly appraised him of the situation.

'Right, I'll get the Commissioner to authorise an Armed Response Unit. You lead the entry into the building from the front and co-ordinate the timings with Red One and let's hope we're not too late.'

Five minutes later three unmarked police Landrovers sped across the city with blue lights flashing and the urgent blare of the emergency horn disturbing the busy London streets. Packham established contact with the ARU who confirmed they were twelve minutes from the bank.

Packham was precise with the instructions, 'Roger that, Red One. Our ETA is fourteen, which is one, four minutes. Get in situ at the end of the service road and wait for my mark for entry. If the doors are closed, just go through them. This is not a hostage situation so let's give them a big surprise.'

'Roger that, Gold One.'

Packham switched channels to his Gold team. 'On arrival, Gold Two disengage the lifts and secure the stairs and reception area. Gold three, proceed to the fourth floor and arrest Bah, Canning and Hall. If they're nor there, find them. I will lead the entry into the service area from the stairs, coordinating with Red One. We don't know how many hostiles to expect, but they will be armed. Preservation of the life of Kell and Solomons is the priority.'

He got the confirmation that everyone understood their roles and looked at watch. It was going to be a long few minutes.

Kell slowly got out of the car with his hands on his head. He moved as slowly as he could, knowing that every second could be the difference between life and death. The fact that Saul was a quivering wreck on the floor of the black cab, was actually a plus. If the bullets started to fly, he was in the best possible place.

Out of the taxi he turned to look at the man in charge who'd been doing all the talking. 'Mr Kell, I've heard all about you. You're quite the hero I understand?'

'Exactly what have you heard, Mr—I didn't catch your name.'

'My name is unimportant. Now, I need you to turn around and put your hands behind your back. My friend here will then secure your hands and lead to our van.'

He looked at Kell, who glanced at the second man holding cable ties. He didn't move.

'I hope you're not going to make this difficult Mr Kell. My employer doesn't want to leave any trace of you or Mr Solomons on this earth. If I have to shoot you here, then technically I'll have failed. But I'm sure Mr Bianchi would understand.'

Kell feigned surprise at hearing Bianchi's name. 'Ah, Mr Bianchi. He won't be very pleased you've let his name slip.'

The man laughed again. 'Dead men don't talk, Mr Kell, now, I won't ask you again, into the van.'

He waited a few moments before slowly turning around and putting his hands behind him. He would only get one opportunity and any chance of success was slim. At that moment, he thought of Amy and all the things she said to him about running headlong into danger, not thinking of the consequences for himself and others.

If he'd just tracked Saul as instructed and reported that he'd met Bianchi, then he'd be sitting in his office with Molly. Young, beautiful, clever and full of life. He knew he was a fool and as he stared into the darkness of his death, he prayed that she'd forgive him. He heard the man with cable ties walking towards him and put his hands by his side. The man stopped. He sensed he was no more than three feet away. A bit too far for what he had planned.

'Mr Kell, I'm out of patience. Either cooperate or die with a bullet in your belly.'

Kell decided it was now or never. 'I'm going to die anyway, so—'

He jumped backwards with all the force he could muster, causing them both to crash to the floor. He went to roll over and jump to his feet only to feel the biting pain of a cable tie crushing his windpipe.

The man with the gun stood over him.

'We are professionals, Mr Kell. Did you really think you could escape from us? Now, Gregor is going to strangle you. This is a good result for me because it won't leave any trace.' He turned and walked over to the taxi as Kell's world started slowly turning black.

The noise was deafening as the armoured car crashed through the shutters and speeded down the ramp into the service area, followed by four armed police running behind it. At the same time, Packham and his team burst out of the stairwell, yelling, 'Armed police, put down your weapons, armed police put down your weapons now!'

Kell felt the pressure on his neck relax and was able to gulp in life-saving breaths of air. No shots were fired as the stunned men dropped their guns and put their hands in the air.

Packham ran to his friend who was trying to sit up having pulled himself away from his strangler, who was being dragged to his feet and handcuffed by one of the Gold team, while the ARU stood guard with their automatic weapons, primed and ready to fire.

'You're alive then,' said Packham.

Kell was breathless but managed. 'What took you so long?' Before slumping to floor. 'Gold Three report,' said Packham.

'All suspects secured. Arrests made.'

'Roger that, Gold Three, good job.'

Saul Solomons emerged from the taxi as Kell was being put into the ambulance. He couldn't take in what had happened. But he was alive. Maybe his luck had finally changed.

35

Wilcox gestured for Bill to sit down at the small table, choosing to sit directly opposite him. The PC stood at the side of the room staring intently at nothing in particular.

'Right, Bill, I want to go over the statement you provided on the day after the fire. I also have further questions following my interview with Roderick Roan. I would point out that at this stage you are not being interviewed under caution and you are free to leave at any time. Do you understand?'

'Why are you saying, "at this stage"?'

'Because, Mr Solomons, "at this stage", you haven't been charged with an offence. If there is evidence that you have committed an offence, then you will be formally cautioned and you can have a solicitor present before you are questioned further. Do you understand?'

'Yes, I understand. You think I did it, don't you?'

'Did what exactly?'

'Started the fire. But I didn't, I swear.'

'Then who did Bill because I'm pretty sure it wasn't young Roddy Roan. So that leaves only you and your brother as the only people with a motive. Now before we continue, is there anything you want to tell me about the night the fire started?'

Bill shook his head.

'OK, let's get back to your original statement.' He flicked through the pages in the folder in front of him, until he found what he was looking for. 'Why didn't you tell us about the hire car?'

'The hire car, er, I didn't think it was relevant.'

'You see the thing is Bill, you led us to believe that had no means of transport as your car was parked at the family home. That meant, apart from getting a taxi or walking six miles across country, you weren't able to return home. In fact, you told me in your original statement that you hadn't been back to the house for the two weeks as your car was out of action. Is that correct?'

'Yes,' he muttered.

Wilcox paused, looking at his suspect, who kept his eyes firmly fixed on the table.

'Bill, lying to the police is a criminal offence. Because I know you went to the house on the night the fire started.'

'You can't know that. You're making it up!'

'I'm not making anything up, Bill. You see, all rental cars have a black box that tracks and records their movements. The insurance insists on it. So when I checked the movements of the Renault you hired, it shows that you drove from the house just after midnight, which is when the fire started. So, I'm going to give you one last chance to tell me the truth or I'll add attempting to pervert the course of justice to the charges you're already facing.'

In barely a whisper, Bill Solomons said. 'It was Saul. He started the fire.' When Wilcox didn't respond, Bill's recounted the events of the fateful evening.

'I was unhappy about how things had been left between us and mother, after the meeting with the solicitors. So, I waited until she would have got to the Eastbourne house and rang her there. It must have been about ten o'clock. She doesn't go to bed particularly early and after the journey, she'd have wanted to unwind. I kept trying but she didn't pick up the phone. You can check my phone if you don't believe me.'

'We already have,' replied Wilcox.

Bill sighed, 'Then you'll know I rang the house at about 11.00 and we had a short conversation. She'd decided to travel down Saturday morning. I asked if I could come over and talk, put things right between us. I felt guilty you see. She's our mother and we shouldn't have started all this trouble over money. She agreed, so I set off at about 11.45 and as I drove up the drive, I could see the flames. When I got out of the car, I saw Saul standing there. I ran up to him and started shaking him by the shoulders. I was screaming at him, *Mother's inside, mother's inside.* And do you know what he said?'

'No Bill, what did he say?'

'I know' and then he got into his car and drove off. I didn't know what to do, the fire was so intense, so I went back to the school. Saul was in his room, lying on the bed. I asked him, why he'd done it. I'll never forget the look on his face when he said, 'Brotherly love, Bill, brotherly love.'

*

The service area in the basement of Streem bank, was a hive of activity as Bianchi's hit team were bundled into the back of separate police vans and the forensic team started a cursory inspection of the area. It wasn't that they were looking for tiny amounts of trace evidence, but simply making sure that nothing obvious was missed. Packham found Saul Solomons sitting on the floor, his knees pulled up to his chin, clearly in shock.

'Come on, Saul, let's get you checked over by the medics, then I'm going to need you to ask you a few questions about what happened this morning.' He hauled Saul to his feet and led him to the remaining ambulance where the paramedic helped him inside. 'I need to take him to the station for questioning, so just a quick check up please.'

He headed over to his team. 'Good work everyone, great job with a great result. Now you know the drill, I need your individual reports by the end of the day. There's a lot going on in this investigation and it has to be by the book.'

Apart from getting Saul back to Police HQ for questioning, he had one final task to perform. He pulled out his mobile and rang Molly.

She answered before he heard the ringtone kick in. 'Chris, is he OK? Is Justin alright?'

'The short answer is yes, he's OK. He's a bit battered and bruised, but he's fine. He's on his way to the Barts to be checked over. It looks like he was separated from his mobile phone, but I'm sure he'll ring you as soon as he can. The best thing for you to do is head over to HQ. That's where we are doing the debrief and trying to pull everything together. It ended up a successful operation Mol, but Justin has some explaining to do as he put his own life and that of Saul

Solomons in danger. Look, I've got to go. I'll catch up with you later.'

The call ended and Molly felt that sick feeling in her stomach. She was getting used to it but didn't like it one bit.

When Packham and the DS walked into the interview room, Saul looked a whole lot better than he did when he got into the ambulance. He had colour in his cheeks and his eyes were clear and alert.

'Now then, Saul, before we start on this morning's events. DS Wilcox would like to ask you about the night of the fire.'

All the colour drained from his face. He looked like he was going to be sick.

Wilcox smiled. 'I've had another chat with your brother and let's say he's had a "road to Damascus" moment. And it's now it's your turn.'

'Whatever he told you, he's lying. I've given you my statement and it's the truth.'

'Your brother states that he drove to the house just after midnight, to find you there, watching the inferno you started. He says he told you that your mother was inside and that you knew this to be the case.'

Both policemen noticed a flicker of uncertainty in the suspect's demeanour.

'The way I see it, it's his word against mine. I didn't go to the house that night. If Bill did go as you say, then he started the fire. He'd been telling me he had this other plan to get hold of the money, not the details mind. I don't think it included murdering our mother but was probably something to do with the insurance.'

Wilcox and Packham looked at each other, wondering where to go next.

'We also have an eyewitness that puts you at the scene.'

Saul laughed, shaking his head. 'You mean that mad student. I don't think so. Look, Bill's taller than me and stockier. We have different haircuts and anyway, it was nighttime. The crazy kid's just making it all up.'

Packham intervened, 'OK, let's leave it there, for the time being. I need to take your statement from this morning. You're facing a long list of charges Saul, so please be honest with me and you never know. There's always a deal to be done.'

Wilcox got up and left, being replaced by a female detective who didn't introduce herself.

36

Molly ignored Packham's advice to go to Police HQ. Instead, she locked up the office and got a taxi to St Bartholomew's hospital. It didn't take long to find the room where Kell was recuperating. It was also slightly disconcerting to see a plain-clothed policeman standing outside.

'Can I see him please?'

'And you are?'

'I'm Molly Cribbs, his girlfriend. I also work for Chris Packham. She held out her Police ID card.'

Visibly relaxing, the policeman said, 'That's fine Molly, in you go, but you'll have to be quick. I'm taking him back to HQ as soon as the doc gives him the all-clear.'

Kell was sitting in a chair at the side of the bed, flicking through a magazine when she walked in. He had a bandage around his neck, but otherwise, he looked fine.

They held each other in a long embrace before Molly gently kissed him on the lips. 'I was so worried darling. What happened? How did you end up with Saul back at the bank.'

Kell let out a huge sigh and sat back down. Molly perched on the edge of the bed, waiting for the explanation.

'I know I'll get a major bollocking from Chris but it's not what you think. I followed Saul and Bianchi down Farringdon

Street to a small park where they sat on a bench, with the American doing all the talking. Saul looked like a broken man. Whatever Bianchi was saying to him was clearly hitting home. No doubt it involved his premature death if he broke ranks on what was going on at Streem.

Suzie Canning had sacked him earlier, so he was a loose end that needed to keep quiet. Anyway, then Bianchi left and I sat with Saul. He told me what had happened and didn't know what to do or where to go. I convinced him he needed to go to the police, so we got the first taxi in a small rank across the road from the park.

The problem was it was one of Bianchi's contracted thugs who was the driver. We drove to the bank and the next thing we're being held at gunpoint, waiting for the clean-up guys to come and finish us off. Chris and the cavalry arrived just in time. Another five minutes and we'd have disappeared. I'm guessing you rang Chris when you saw Saul's tracker heading to the bank.'

'Yes, but after that, it was awful with nothing to do but wait.'

She felt slightly better that it wasn't the case that he'd been all gung ho and gone charging in to save the day. But he had gone further than sticking to just his watching brief.

At that moment, the doctor came in, followed by the plain-clothed policeman. He shone a light into Kell's eyes, asked him a couple of questions before saying, 'You're fine, Mr Kell. You might need painkillers for a couple of days, but paracetamol and ibuprofen will be fine. You're good to go.'

Nobody spoke as they drove across London to Police HQ. Kell and Molly sat in the back holding hands, lost in their own thoughts.

There were no security checks when they arrived. They were led straight to the meeting room they'd been to before, where Packham was in full flow. He paused as they found their seats and finished his briefing on what had occurred underneath the bank.

'For once, Justin, your timing is perfect. Please can you illuminate us as to what happened earlier and why you failed to follow my instructions?'

Kell felt the bandage on this neck. 'Thanks, Chris, your concern is touching.'

Packham managed a grin and nodded to him to continue. Kell repeated everything he'd told Molly, adding detail when he was questioned on a specific. When he finished, Packham asked the room if there were any more questions.

One of the security services guys asked, 'What were the exact words Canning used regarding Bianchi's men?'

'Please try and be patient. Mr Bianchi's colleagues will be here shortly,' replied Kell.

'It's probably not enough to detain him, but I'll pass it on.' The spook got up and left the room.

The meeting broke up after the plan for interviewing the executives from Streem was agreed. They'd all lawyered up and were waiting to be questioned. Packham gestured to Kell and Molly to remain behind while the others filed out of the room.

'You just about got away with that. They were all keen to see you strung up and to never darken our doors again. However, they all recognise that they'd have done the same in your position. It's a great result for us. A major laundering operation has been closed down. Bah, Hall and Canning should be put away for at least ten years and we should recover millions in dirty money.'

'What will happen to the school?' asked Molly.

'The view is the sale was illegal, due to the nature of the funds. These will be recovered, so the original shareholders will be back in charge, but it will take time. I doubt they'll be opening until next year. My guys will focus on getting the money back and Wilcox is close to making an arrest re the fire, but it's hit a stumbling block.'

'Why is that?' asked Kell.

'Both brothers are saying it was the other one who started the fire. The evidence is mostly circumstantial, with the only witness being one of the pupils. Apparently, he's not exactly reliable. Anyway, as Saul Solomons is a key witness and suspect in the bank investigation, Wilcox is having the other brother brought to be held here, while he sorts it all out. He'll be interested in what you've got to say re Saul, so if you can hang around I'll send him up when he's free. Now, I've got to crack on. Make yourselves comfortable.'

37

Wilcox walked into the room an hour later. He had the look of a man who needed a shower and a clean set of clothes. Following brief introductions, Wilcox took off his jacket, put it on the back of a chair, sat down and opened his notebook.

'Right. Saul Solomons, what can you tell me?'

'Before I do that, would you mind filling us in on what you've got so far?' asked Kell.

'Seriously?'

'If you wouldn't mind. Then we've all got the full picture.' Kell tried his most engaging smile, causing Wilcox to laugh.

'Yeh, sure. I need all the help I can get on this one. Is he always this charming?' he asked Molly.

'Not all the time, but he has his moments!'

Wilcox ran through the details of the case and the interviews with Bill, Saul and Roddy.

Kell took it all in, processing what he'd heard. 'As you know I've spent a bit of time with Saul and I don't believe he is capable of starting the fire and murdering his mother. Up until a few weeks ago, he had a good job and a gambling problem. Then fate puts him in the middle of a major money laundering operation, the murder of Emile Black, the previous incumbent of his new role and threats from an American mafia family that he's a dead man if he steps out of line. He's a weak character is Saul. Not a murderer.

On the other hand, you've got the older brother Bill. Still living with his mum, issues with her and at work. He's thrust into a world he knows nothing about but suddenly can see a way out of his mundane life. He desperately wants to be accepted and a part of the criminal operation. He needs to find £1m along with his brother, but unlike Saul, it instantly becomes an obsession. He knows there's money in the family and the fact that he can't get his hands on it is making him mad.

Saul's got his own problems, which for him are the priority. But…Bill's story doesn't add up. Ringing the house at 11.00 PM and arranging to go over to speak to his mum. Why the urgency? Then it takes him 45 minutes before he sets off? What was he doing? When he does get there and sees the house ablaze, why doesn't he ring the fire brigade? No, he goes back to bed, possibly via his brother's room and the next day plays the shocked son when he hears what's happened.'

Kell started pacing around the room, working through the sequence of events. 'Then we come to Saul. He's the one that phones the Eastbourne house, he's the one who drives down there. Hardly the actions of someone who knows his mum has just burned to death. So he's either innocent or they're in it together. But my conclusion is that Bill is your man. It's circumstantial, but he'll crack if pushed hard enough.'

Wilcox stood up, stretching out his back. 'It pains me to say this, but good job, Mr Kell. Now, I've a few more needles to stick into Bill Solomon, together with a major change in approach.'

Bill Solomons was fidgeting with his phone, checking the same emails he'd read ten times already as he waited for Wilcox to reappear. He was starting to feel claustrophobic in the small room, desperate to get outside and some fresh air. When Wilcox walked in, his sidekick dutifully following, he sensed a shift in the atmosphere.

'William Solomons, I'm charging you with arson at your family home on the 15 and 16 August. You are charged with the murder of your mother, Mrs Esther Solomons on the same dates and for attempting to pervert the course of justice. You do not have to say anything, but it may harm your defence if you do not mention when questioned something which you later rely on in court. Anything you do say may be given in evidence. I suggest you use your phone call to get your solicitor down here pronto.'

A stunned Bill Solomons realised it would be some time before he'd be out in the fresh air again.

It took Miles Crabtree a couple of hours to get down to London. A policeman let him into the interview room where he found Bill with his head resting on his arms on the table. 'Right, Bill, what's all this nonsense about?'

He looked up with tears in his eyes. 'It's not nonsense, Miles. It's true. I killed my mother.'

'Wow, I wasn't expecting that. You'd better start from the beginning.'

It took Bill over an hour to tell the story of the ongoing battle with his mother for the money he knew was his. How the sale of the school had brought things to a head when he was given the opportunity to invest, his brother's link with the Streem bank and the corruption that he'd found himself involved with. When he'd finished, his solicitor asked.

'Did Saul know what you were planning. What you did?'

He shook his head. 'No, I lied to the police saying that it was Saul that started the fire. But he didn't know or do anything.'

'What evidence do the police have?'

'I'm not sure. But in between going through my statement again and a couple of hours later, they must have found something because that's when they charged me. Anyway, it doesn't matter about the evidence. It's true. I burned our home down, knowing mother was inside. I deserve to die, Miles, but instead I'll rot in prison for the rest of my life.'

'So you intend to admit your guilt before you hear what they've got on you?'

In barely a whisper, 'Yes. I can't take anymore.'

Epilogue

Al and Roddy sat on their trunks outside the main entrance waiting for their parents to come and pick them up from The Wellington School for the final time. It was a warm late summer morning, the silence between them only disturbed by the birdsong that mingled with the light breeze.

'You're definitely going to take a year out then?' Al asked his friend.

'Yes, it's for the best. I need to sort myself out,' replied Roddy, who with his close-cropped hair and a bit of colour in his cheeks reminded Al of the boy when he first met him. 'Do you know what's going to happen to this place?' asked Roddy.

Al shook his head. 'Apparently, it's going to take some time to sort out the financial situation. Then it's a case of finding someone to buy the place and whether they think it's possible to relaunch the school. My guess is the land will be sold for development, but it'll be a couple of years before it's all sorted.'

'I hope it does become a school again,' mused Roddy. 'Despite everything, we had some great times here, didn't we? And if it does stay as a school I might come back to finish my A levels.'

Al looked at his friend and smiled. 'Sure, that would be a good thing to do. But sadly I won't be joining you. I'm going to the local grammar school to finish up the sixth form and then hopefully off to Uni.' He stood up and kicked at the gravel driveway. 'More importantly, what are you going to do in the meantime?'

'I'm going to live with my uncle, down in Cornwall. He's got a small farm and I'll work there until I decide what to do next. The fresh air and outdoor life will do me good. I got too bogged down in my studies here, took everything a bit too seriously.'

'No counselling then?

'No. I had a couple of sessions with the police psychologist and they decided I wasn't that mad after all!' He turned at looked at Al.

'Do you, think I'm mad Al?'

'No my friend. You are just a bit different and there's nothing wrong with that.'

They were distracted by the sound a car coming up the long driveway. They instinctively hugged, neither seeing the tears in the other's eye.

*

Kell and Molly sat in the office preparing to sift through the latest batch of CVs in the increasingly frustrating search to find someone who they thought would fit in at the firm.

'I'm struggling to find the motivation to do this. I mean after the excitement of the last case, it's all very mundane,' said Molly.

'I know what you mean, but we've got to sort this and quickly. The contract with the Met means you're working for them for two and half days a week. There's no way I can manage our caseload on my own.'

He paused, putting down the pile of paper he'd just picked up.

'There's also another thing I've been thinking about as far as the company is concerned. It's relevant for the recruitment and it's about your position.'

'Ooh, am I getting a pay rise and a fancy new title?'

Kell laughed. 'You could say that. You are far more than just an employee here. We're a partnership outside of work and to all intents and purposes, we are in work as well. I think it's important that anyone who we employ understands that and that you're not just an "employee". JK Investigations Ltd is a limited company and I hold all of the shares. What I propose is that we make you a director and give you a shareholding of say 33 per cent. It helps from a tax perspective, but more importantly, it means you're officially an integral part of the business. So, what do you say?'

She got up, kissed him gently on the lips, looking into his eyes as they hugged.

Kell's mobile rang, breaking the moment. He saw it was Packham. 'Chis, what's occurring?'

'Thought you'd like to know, we had to let Bianchi go. We knew we didn't have anything on him and he's not breathing a word about Streem or any of the related investigations. He's on his way back to the airport as we speak.'

'Well, it's what we expected. Disappointing, but he's a sharp operator and that was always going to happen. I don't think he'll be keen to come back here anytime soon.'

Packham continued, 'The CPS have offered a deal to Saul Solomons. Everything he knows about what went on at Streem, for a free ride on the money laundering charges. He'll be given a new ID and relocated, so not a bad result from what he could have been facing. He's also going to inherit the family estate. Bill has already signed over his share before the court stopped him inheriting.'

'What about Emile Black, are they charging Bah and Canning with his murder?' asked Kell.

'It's still being worked on, but it looks likely. Suzie Canning is desperately trying to do a deal, but the CPS aren't interested as the evidence is overwhelming.'

'OK, thanks for the update, Chris. Keep me posted.'

He ended the call.

'They've let John Bianchi go. Nothing they could hold him on. And Saul's got his get out of jail free card, for his evidence against Bah and his cronies.'

Molly was distracted, 'OK, now where were we.'

'Sorry, I thought you'd be interested. But anyway, I was telling you about your newfound status as a director of the business. So, what do you say Miss Cribbs.'

'I love you, Justin Kell, whether or not I'm an employee or a director, shareholder or whatever. If you think this is for the best, then, I'm absolutely delighted.' She led him back to the meeting table and they sat down next to each other. 'Now, I've got some news of my own.'

She didn't immediately say what it was, but simply looked at him, a pensive smile on her face.

Finally, she said, 'I'm pregnant. I hope that's OK?'

Kell froze. 'What? But I thought. How long?' The words came incoherently.

She held his hands and looked lovingly into his eyes. 'I didn't plan it, darling. It was an accident. I've known for over a week, but with everything going on, I couldn't find the right time to tell you. Are you OK?'

'Er, yes. I'm fine. No, I'm not fine, I'm overjoyed. It's wonderful. I don't what to say.'

Tears of joy trickled down his face.

'There is one thing,' she paused, trying to find the right words. 'It changes everything. A baby. We both will have enormous responsibilities and I'm worried about you. About how you ignore the rules, ignore advice, even when it's Chris or the police telling you. You could have gotten yourself killed at Streem. If the police had been five minutes later, then you and Saul Solomons would be dead and our baby would be without a father. It's not fair to bring a baby into a life like that. You understand what I'm saying?'

The tears were coming faster and he sobbed into her shoulder as they hugged.

'I do understand and I promise I'll change. I'll go back to being a journalist if I have to. I love you, Molly Cribbs, and I'll love the baby with everything I have.'

She closed her eyes, trying to believe him.

THE END

Ingram Content Group UK Ltd.
Milton Keynes UK
UKHW020641220623
423865UK00012B/596